THE WIZARDS' DEN

THE WIZARDS' DEN

Spellbinding Stories of Magic and Magicians

Edited by

PETER HAINING

SOUVENIR PRESS

Copyright © 2001 by Seventh Zenith Ltd.

The right of Peter Haining to be identified as editor of
this work has been asserted by him in accordance with the
Copyright, Designs and Patents Act 1988.

First published 2001 by
Souvenir Press Ltd.,
43 Great Russell Street, London WC1B 3PD

ISBN 0 285 63628 6

Typeset by Rowland Phototypesetting Ltd,
Bury St Edmunds, Suffolk

Printed in Great Britain by
Creative Print & Design, Wales, Ebbw Vale

This book is for
JAMES, CHARLIE & BEN
Three Little Wizards

Off to some shadowy glen where wizards
their mystic charms prepare.

ANN RADCLIFFE
The Mysteries of Udolpho (1794)

Magic has a universal appeal.

J. K. ROWLING
Reader's Digest (December 2001)

CONTENTS

THE WORLD OF WIZARDRY

If you go to the little village of Corris in the valley of the great Welsh mountain, Cader Idris, you will find the entrance to some vast caverns known as King Arthur's Labyrinth. Inside sits a boy wizard called Myrddin, more popularly known as Merlin, who once foretold the coming of the warrior king, Arthur, and predicted a battle between a white dragon and a red dragon for the future of the Welsh nation. The clever-looking, blond-haired boy in his sack-cloth tunic is not real, of course, but a life-like model of just one of the many wizards who have for generations being practising their ancient art of magic. For, you see, wizards *are* real and not just imaginary characters from the minds of storytellers like T. H. White, J. R. R. Tolkien and, most recently, J. K. Rowling.

The fact of the matter is that wizards have been around for centuries. They are referred to in the Bible—Chapter 19 of Isaiah mentions 'wizards'—and you can find them in the poems of John Milton who talks about 'star-led wizards . . . with odours sweet' and in Shakespeare's play, *The Tempest*, featuring the sorcerer, Prospero. Mostly they are described as older men: tall, bearded, with flowing hair, wearing long cloaks decorated with mystic symbols and carrying magic wands. There are female wizards, too, known as wizardesses, and one is famously referred to by

Percy Shelley in his fantasy, *The Witch of Atlas,* in the words, 'All day the wizard lady sat aloof, spelling out scrolls of dread antiquity'. Each and every one of these people, though, began learning to be wizards when they were young—and not a few have subsequently become the focus of myths and legends as well as the inspiration for stories. In the past, these magic-makers were always spoken about in whispers with a mixture of fear and respect; today they may well be known familiarly as a 'wiz'.

So, what is a wizard? According to the dictionaries they are people who are skilled in the occult arts and practise magic and witchcraft. They are also wise, can see into the future, and hypnotise ordinary folk. They have been schooled in sorcery and conjuring and have a language of their own which is far removed from the common expressions usually associated with wizardry like *Abracadabra!* and *Open Sesame!* Wizards live in a world where just about anything is possible: they can change their appearance—a skill known as 'shape shifting'—transfigure all kinds of inanimate objects and even become invisible. They can see ghosts, summon up supernatural powers, and create great happiness or work terrible vengeance. But wizards are not bad—though when some of their number have been exposed to the temptations of magic they have misused it—and they do not necessarily use their powers to inflict injury. Though they *can* do so when battling with evil people and deadly creatures or when locked in struggles with the forces of darkness.

One of the first history books about wizards was called *The Wizard Unvisored* and it was written in 1652.

No one knows who the author was, though it is believed he may well have been a wizard because of all the information the book contains about the secret art. It even lists a number of wizards who were said to be working magic in London at that time. There was 'the cunning man' on Bankside, a 'shaggy-haired wizard' in Pepper Alley, and 'Doctor Forman' with his 'bag-pipe cheek' of Lambeth. Even more intriguing was Mother Broughton in Chick Lane and young Master Oliver who lived in Turnbull Street. He had obviously been a good pupil and learned the art of wizardry quicker than most. Although little is known about Oliver beyond his name, he was part of an already ancient tradition and a forerunner of some of the young wizards to be found in this book.

A traditional wizard raising some curious spirits in his magic circle.

Sadly, although *The Wizard Unvisored* had a picture of a wizard at work in his magic circle, there was no portrait of the remarkable Master Oliver.

However, a great deal more *is* known about the boy wizard Merlin who grew up to be probably the most famous magic-maker in history. The facts about his life are, it is true, steeped in mystery, but he is believed to have lived late in the sixth century AD. He is said to have been 'a boy without a father' who grew up in Carmarthen, studying magic with a famous wizard, Blaise of Brittany. It was in Wales that Merlin first began to earn his reputation as a prophet when he predicted the coming of King Arthur. He also offered guidance to the Welsh King Gwrtheyrn, when the monarch was trying to build a castle at Dinas Emrys. Merlin said this would never succeed because two dragons, one white and one red, lay sleeping in a subterranean lake below the site. When Gwrtheyrn ordered the lake to be drained, the two dragons awoke and began fighting until the red one finally triumphed. Although Gwrtheyrn was still unable to build his fortress, the events are said to be the reason why the red dragon became the national emblem of Wales. Today, Bryn Myrddin, 'Merlin's Hill,' in Carmarthen commemorates the wizard's younger days and is rumoured to be the place where he still sleeps—imprisoned, it is said, for revealing some of his magic secrets. A local legend claims Merlin's 'ghostly wailings' can sometimes be heard on dark, stormy nights issuing from deep inside the hill.

Merlin is also associated with Cornwall, where he settled after years of wandering the countryside with only a wild pig as his companion. There, at Tintagel

Castle, it is said the boy Arthur was born, destined to be one of the greatest English kings, and Merlin used his magic to become an invaluable member of the court and ally to the famous Knights of the Round Table. According to another legend, the wizard employed his powers to transport the giant stones which now form Stonehenge from their original home in Ireland. They were tied together, flown over the Irish Sea to Salisbury Plain, and there laid out according to Merlin's plan. Memories of the great wizard are kept alive at Tintagel by a cavern below the clifftop castle which is known as 'Merlin's Cave', and also in the pages of the classic fantasy novel, *The Sword in the Stone* by T. H. White, which retells the

Merlin, with his pupil, the young King Arthur, meet the Lady of the Lake.

story of Arthur's childhood and the wizard's role as his tutor.

In the North of England, at Alderley Edge, a sheer sandstone cliff rising from the Cheshire plain, can be found a wishing well that is also associated with Merlin. The well, formed by a natural spring, carries an inscription which reads:

Drink of this and take thy fill,
For the water falls by the wizard's will.

Merlin is believed to have performed one of his great feats of magic here, throwing open some massive gates concealed in the rock face to reveal a huge cavern. There lay King Arthur and his knights asleep, awaiting the call when the people of England again needed their courage and bravery. This legend has been utilised in the famous novel, *The Weirdstone of Brisingamen* by Alan Garner, who has contributed this book.

Scotland has its stories of wizards, too. In Selkirk stands Oakwood Tower, the home of Michael Scot, who is said to have compiled a volume of spells and incantations known as the *Book of Might*. Scot lived during the early years of the thirteenth century and learned the secrets of wizardry in Paris. Legend has it that he was a brilliant astrologer and seer and such was his control of magic that he once flew to France mounted on a demon horse. The *Book of Might* is believed to have been buried with him in Melrose Abbey. Much closer to our own times, in the eighteenth century, another Scotsman, Alexander Skene, went to Italy as a teenager to learn all about becoming a wizard. When he returned to Aberdeen and lived at what is now called Skene House, such were his magical powers that he became known far and wide as 'The Wizard Laird'. It is said that he never cast a shadow even in the brightest sunlight and travelled everywhere with four birds—a crow, a hawk, a magpie and a jackdaw—which he referred to as 'my imps'. He was skilled at creating magic potions from herbs collected in the local glens and used these against a number of evil-doers. Thrilling stories of 'The Wizard Laird' are still repeated in the Aberdeen district to this day.

Another famous Scottish folk story, 'The Wizard's

A lesson in magic-making at The Great Wizard's College of Magic.

Apprentice' collected by J. F. Campbell and published in his *Popular Tales of the West Highlands* in
1860, tells the story of a young farmer's son who was
trained in the ways of magic by a wizard, Fiachaire
Gobha. The boy learned to cast spells and also to
become a 'shape-shifter' turning into a dog, a bull,
a horse and even a pair of bellows in one strange
incident. But what makes this tale particularly interesting is its reference to the 'Great Wizard's College
of Magic' which the old man had attended and to
which he sent his young pupil. There is very little
actual information about the college in the story,
although there is a suggestion it may have been
located in Italy and was perhaps the same establish-
ment that Alexander Skene attended. More likely, it
was in Scotland, probably in a remote corner of the
western Highlands. In any event, it can be seen as
a forerunner of Harry Potter's Hogwarts School of
Witchcraft and Wizardry which is also located in a
remote Scottish castle.

Evidence of wizards can be found in other places,
too. Sometimes they appear to have frightened
people so much that a number suffered the same
fate as Thomas Sche who, in 1596, was burned at the
stake. There is an account of a trial in 1751 which
reports, 'A large mob at Tring [in Hertfordshire]
declared revenge against Osborne and his wife as a
wizard and witch', and a century later the author,
William Hone, in his *Every-day Book* reports that, in
July 1825, 'a man was swam for a wizard at Wickham
Skeith in Suffolk'. Other writers speak more favour-
ably about the activities of wizards including Henry
Mayhew in his work *London Labour and the London*

Poor (1851–62) who quotes one man: 'I call myself a wizard which means conjuror, astrologer and fortune teller.' Three famous nineteenth-century wizards are also featured in works of fiction: Sir Walter Scott describes 'Lord Gifford in his wizard habit strange' in *Marmion* (1808); the Dutch-born wizard, Gerald Dow, is mentioned practising his art in America by Nathaniel Hawthorne in *Tanglewood Tales* (1853) and Rudyard Kipling refers in *Life's Handicap* (1891) to, 'Juseen Daze, the wizard-man, who keeps the "Talking Monkey's Head"'.

Wizards of all ages have continued to appear in modern fiction, too. In 1900, little Dorothy set out

The modern wizard, Professor De Lara, and a potential young client.

to find *The Wonderful Wizard of Oz* in the story by L. Frank Baum. She was followed in 1938 by T. H. White's *The Sword in the Stone*, featuring the boy Wart who is taught the ways of magic by Merlin and metamorphosed into the shape of various animals to learn their ways. Wart has been described as a spiritual ancestor of Harry Potter, a verdict with which anyone who reads the book will probably agree. Merlin reappeared in *That Hideous Strength* by C. S. Lewis (1945). In 1968, J. R. R. Tolkien introduced another wonderful character, the wizard Gandalf, in his *The Lord of the Rings*. In their footsteps has arrived J. K. Rowling's versatile young Harry Potter, the trainee wizard at Hogwarts School, continuing the tradition of wizardry in fact and fiction that has proved so fascinating to readers of all ages.

I very much hope that the stories about this long-standing tradition which I have chosen for this book—beginning with 'Professor De Lara and the Twopenny Spell' by E. Nesbit, the writer who, J. K. Rowling has admitted, greatly influenced her—will transport you to the world of wizardry where anything, and I do mean *anything*, is possible. And, hopefully, if the magic is not *too* powerful, allow you to return safely . . .

PETER HAINING
Dolgellau, Wales
April 2001

THE WIZARDS' DEN

PROFESSOR DE LARA AND THE TWOPENNY SPELL

E. Nesbit

Professor Doloro de Lara—to give him his full name—is a Wizard of Magic (White) and the Black Art. He is very tall and rather scary-looking with black eyes and what some people who have met him call an indescribable mouth. He can also change his appearance in a flash. The professor's advertisements say that he will instruct young pupils in their own homes—at no extra charge—and he offers 'Special Terms for Schools'. He could almost be a member of the staff of Harry Potter's school, Hogwarts, which is not such a surprise because as a child J. K. Rowling was very impressed by the books of E. Nesbit. She, too, was an author who wrote about wizards and magic and preferred to sign her work with just an initial. In this story, a little girl named Lucy wants Professor de Lara to give her a spell to teach her bullying brother, Harry, a lesson. But the wizard's magic has a rather unexpected result, as you will discover . . .

*   *   *

Lucy was a very good little girl indeed, and Harry was not so bad—for a boy, though the grown-ups called him a scamp! They both got on very well at school, and were not wholly unloved at home. Perhaps Lucy was a bit of a duffer, and Harry was certainly very rude to call her one, but she need not have replied by calling him a 'beast.' I think she did it partly to show him that she was not quite so much of a duffer as he thought, and partly because she was naturally annoyed at being buried up to her waist in the ground among the gooseberry-bushes. She got into the hole Harry had dug because he said it might make her grow, and then he suddenly shovelled down a heap of earth and stamped it down so that she could not move. She began to cry, then he said duffer and she said 'beast,' and he went away and left her 'planted there,' as the French people say. And she cried more than ever, and tried to dig herself out, and couldn't, and although she was naturally such a gentle child, she would have stamped with rage, only she couldn't get her feet out to do it. Then she screamed, and her Uncle Richard came and dug her out, and said it was a shame, and gave her twopence to spend as she liked. So she got nurse to clean the gooseberry ground off her, and when she was cleaned she went out to spend the twopence. She was allowed to go alone, because the shops were only a little way off on the same side of the road, so there was no danger from crossings.

'I'll spend every penny of it on myself,' said Lucy savagely; 'Harry shan't have a bit, unless I could think of something he wouldn't like, and then I'd get it and put it in his bread and milk!' She had never felt quite so spiteful before, but, then, Harry had never before been quite so aggravating.

She walked slowly along by the shops, wishing she could think of something that Harry hated; she herself hated worms, but Harry didn't mind them. Boys are so odd.

Suddenly she saw a shop she had never noticed before. The window was quite full of flowers—roses, lilies, violets, pinks, pansies—everything you can think of, growing in a tangled heap, as you see them in an old garden in July.

She looked for the name over the shop. Instead of being somebody or other, Florist, it was 'Doloro de Lara, Professor of white and black Magic,' and in the window was a large card, framed and glazed. It said:

ENCHANTMENTS DONE WHILE YOU WAIT.
EVERY DESCRIPTION OF CHARM
CAREFULLY AND COMPETENTLY WORKED.
STRONG SPELLS FROM FIFTY GUINEAS
TO TWO PENCE.
WE SUIT ALL PURSES.
GIVE US A TRIAL.
BEST AND CHEAPEST HOUSE IN THE TRADE.
COMPETITION DEFIED.

Lucy read this with her thumb in her mouth. It was the twopence that attracted her; she had never bought a spell, and even a twopenny one would be something new.

'It's some sort of conjuring trick, I suppose,' she thought, 'and I'll never let Harry see how it's done—never, never, never!'

She went in. The shop was just as flowery, and bowery, and red-rosy, and white-lilyish inside as out, and the colour and the scent almost took her breath away. A thin, dark, unpleasing gentleman suddenly popped out of a bower of flowering nightshade, and said:

'And what can we do for you to-day, miss?'

'I want a spell, if you please,' said Lucy; 'the best you can do for twopence.'

'Is that all you've got?' said he.

'Yes,' said Lucy.

'Well, you can't expect much of a spell for that,' said he; 'however, it's better that I should have the twopence than that you should; you see that, of course. Now, what would you like? We can do you a nice little spell at sixpence that'll make it always jam for tea. And I've another article at eighteenpence that'll make the grown-ups always think you're good even if you're not; and at half a crown —'

'I've only got twopence.'

'Well,' he said crossly, 'there's only one spell at that price, and that's really a twopenny-half-penny one; but we'll say twopence. I can make you like somebody else, and somebody else like you.'

'Thank you,' said Lucy; 'I like most people, and everybody likes me.'

'I don't mean *that*,' he said. 'Isn't there someone you'd like to hurt if you were as strong as they are, and they were as weak as you?'

'Yes,' said Lucy in a guilty whisper.

'Then hand over your twopence,' said the dark gentleman, 'and it's a bargain.'

He snatched the coppers warm from her hand.

'Now,' he said, 'to-morrow morning you'll be as strong as Harry, and he'll be little and weak like you. Then you can hurt him as much as you like, and he won't be able to hurt back.'

'Oh!' said Lucy; 'but I'm not sure I want—I think I'd like to change the spell, please.'

'No goods exchanged,' he said crossly; 'you've got what you asked for.'

'Thank you,' said Lucy doubtfully, 'but how am I—?'

'It's entirely self-adjusting,' said nasty Mr Doloro. 'No previous experience required.'

'Thank you very much,' said Lucy. 'Good—

She was going to say 'good-morning,' but it turned into 'good gracious,' because she was so very much astonished. For, without a moment's warning, the flower-shop had turned into the sweet-shop that she knew so well, and nasty Mr Doloro had turned into the sweet-woman, who was asking what she wanted, to which, of course, as she had spent her twopence, the answer was 'Nothing.' She was already sorry that she had spent it, and in such a way, and she was sorrier still when she got home, and Harry owned handsomely that *he* was sorry he had planted her out, but he really hadn't thought she was such a little idiot, and he *was* sorry—so there! This touched Lucy's heart, and she felt more than ever that she had not laid out her twopence to the best advantage. She tried to warn Harry of what was to happen in the morning, but he only said, 'Don't yarn; Billson Minor's coming for cricket. You can field if you like.' Lucy didn't like, but it seemed the only thing she could do to show that she accepted in a proper spirit her brother's apology about the planting out. So she fielded gloomily and ineffectively.

Next morning Harry got up in good time, folded up his nightshirt, and made his room so tidy that the housemaid nearly had a surprise-fit when she went in. He crept downstairs like a mouse, and learned his lessons before breakfast. Lucy, on the other hand, got up so late that it was only by dressing hastily that she had time to prepare a thoroughly good booby-trap before she slid down the banisters just as the breakfast-bell rang. She was first in the room, so she was able to put a little salt in all the tea-cups before anyone else came in. Fresh tea was made, and Harry was blamed. Lucy said, 'I did it,' but no one believed her. They said she was a noble, unselfish sister to try and shield her naughty brother, and Harry burst into floods of tears when she kicked him under the table; she hated herself for doing this, but somehow it seemed impossible to do anything else.

Harry cried nearly all the way to school, while Lucy insisted on sliding along all the gutters and dragging Harry after her. She bought a catapult at the toy-shop and a pennyworth of tintacks at the oil-shop, both on credit, and as Lucy had never asked for credit before, she got it.

At the top of Blackheath Village they separated— Harry went back to his school, which is at the other side of the station, and Lucy went on to the High School.

The Blackheath High School has a large and beautiful hall, with a staircase leading down into it like a staircase in a picture, and at the other end of the hall is a big statue of a beautiful lady. The High School mistresses call her Venus, but I don't really believe that is her name.

Lucy—good, gentle, little Lucy, beloved by her form mistress and respected by all the school—sat on those steps—I don't know why no one caught her—and used her catapult to throw ink pellets (you know what they are, of course) with her catapult at the beautiful white statue-lady, till the Venus—if that is her name, which I doubt—was all over black spots, like a Dalmation or carriage dog.

Then she went into her class room and arranged tintacks, with the business end up, on all the desks and seats, an act fraught with gloomy returns to Blossoma Rand and Wilhelmina Marguerite Asterisk. Another booby-trap—a dictionary, a pot of water, three pieces of chalk, and a handful of torn paper— was hastily sketched above the door. Three other little girls looked on in open-mouthed appreciation. I do not wish to shock you, so I will not tell you about the complete success of the booby-trap, nor of the bloodthirsty fight between Lucy and Bertha Kaurter in a secluded fives-court during rec. Dora Spielman and Gertrude Rook were agitated seconds. It was Lucy's form mistress, the adored Miss Harter Larke, who interrupted the fight at the fifth round, and led the blood-stained culprits into the hall and up the beautiful picture-like steps to the Headmistress's room.

The Head of the Blackheath High School has all the subtle generalship of the Head in Mr Kipling's *Stalky*. She has also a manner which subdues parents and children alike to 'what she works in, like the dyer's hand.' Anyone less clever would have expelled the luckless Lucy—saddled with her brother's boy-nature—on such evidence as was now brought forward. Not so the Blackheath Head. She reserved judgment, the most terrible of all things for a culprit, by the way, who thought it over for an hour and a half in the mistress's room, and she privately wrote a note to Lucy's mother, gently hinting that Lucy was not quite herself: might be sickening for something. Perhaps she had better be kept at home for a day or two. Lucy went home, and on the way upset a bicycle with a little girl on it, and came off best in a heated physical argument with a baker's boy.

Harry, meanwhile, had dried his tears, and gone to school. He knew his lessons, which was a strange and pleasing thing, and roused in his master hopes destined to be firmly and thoroughly crushed in the near future. But when he had emerged triumphantly from morning school he suddenly found his head being punched by Simpkins Minor, on the ground that he, Harry, had been showing off. The punching was scientific and irresistible. Harry, indeed, did not try to resist; in floods of tears and with uncontrolled emotion he implored Simpkins Minor to let him alone, and not be a brute. Then Simpkins Minor kicked him, and several other nice little boy-friends of his joined the glad throng, and it became quite a kicking party. So that when Harry and Lucy met at the corner of Wemyss Road his face was almost unrecognisable, while Lucy looked as happy as a king, and as proud as a peacock.

'What's up?' asked Lucy briskly.

'Every single boy in the school has kicked me,' said Harry in flat accents. 'I wish I was dead.'

'So do I,' said Lucy cheerily; 'I think I'm going to be expelled. I should be quite certain, only my booby-trap came down on Bessie Jayne's head instead of Miss Whatshername's, and Bessie's no sneak, though she has got a lump like an ostrich's egg on her forehead, and soaked through as well. But I think I'm certain to be expelled.'

'I wish I was,' said Harry, weeping with heartfelt emotion. 'I don't know what's the matter with me; I feel all wrong inside. Do you think you can turn into things just by reading them? Because I feel as if I was in *Sandford and Merton*, or one of the books the kind clergyman lent us at the seaside.'

'How awfully beastly!' said Lucy. 'Now, I feel as if I didn't care twopence whether I was expelled or not. And, I say, Harry, I feel as if I was much stronger than you. I know I could twist your arm round and then hit it like you did me the other day, and you couldn't stop me.'

'Of course I couldn't! *I* can't stop anybody doing anything they want to do. Anybody who likes can hit me, and I can't hit back.'

He began to cry again. And suddenly Lucy was really sorry. She had done this, she had degraded her happy brother to a mere milksop, just because he had happened to plant her out, and leave her planted. Remorse suddenly gripped her with tooth and claw.

'Look here,' she said, 'it's all my fault! Because you planted me out, and I wanted to hurt you. But now I don't. I can't make you boy-brave again; but I'm sorry, and I'll look after you, Harry, old man! Perhaps you could disguise yourself in frocks and long hair, and come to the High School. I'd take care nobody bullied you. It isn't nice being bullied, is it?'

Harry flung his arms round her, a thing he would never have done in the public street if he had not been girlish inside at the time.

'No, it's hateful,' he said. 'Lucy, I'm sorry I've been such a pig to you.'

Lucy put her arms round him, and they kissed each other, though it was broad daylight and they were walking down Lee Park.

The same moment the enchanter Doloro de Lara ran into them on the pavement. Lucy screamed, and Harry hit out as hard as he could.

'Look out,' said he; 'who are you shoving into?'

'Tut-tut,' said the enchanter, putting his hat straight, 'you've bust up your spell, my Lucy—child; no spells hold if you go kissing and saying you're sorry. Just keep that in mind for the future, will you?'

He vanished in the white cloud of a passing steam-motor, and Harry and Lucy were left looking at each other. And Harry was Harry and Lucy was Lucy to the very marrow of their little back-bones. They shook hands with earnest feeling.

Next day Lucy went to the High School and apologised in dust and ashes.

'I don't think I was my right self,' she said to the Headmistress, who quite agreed with her, 'and I never will again!'

And she never has. Harry, on the other hand, thrashed Simpkins Minor thoroughly and scientifically on the first opportunity; but he did not thrash him extravagantly: he tempered pluck with mercy.

For this is the odd thing about the whole story. Ever since the day when the twopenny spell did its work Harry has been kinder than before and Lucy braver. I can't think why, but so it is. He no longer bullies her, and she is no longer afraid of him, and every time she does something brave for him, or he does something kind for her, they grow more and more alike, so that when they are grown up he may as well be called Lucius and she Harriett, for all the difference there will be between them.

And all the grown-ups look on and admire, and think that their incessant jawing has produced this improvement. And no one suspects the truth except the Headmistress of the High School who has gone through the complete course of Social Magic under a better professor than Mr Doloro de Lara; that is why she understands everything, and why she did not expel Lucy, but only admonished her. Harry is cock of his school now, and Lucy is in the sixth, and a model girl. I wish all Headmistresses learned Magic at Girton.

*　　*　　*

E. NESBIT—the 'E' stands for Edith—was probably the first really modern children's author. Her fantasy stories, written during the early years of the twentieth century, have been very influential on many storytellers, notably J. K. Rowling who says, 'I identify with Nesbit more than any other writer. She said that, by some lucky chance, she remembered exactly how she felt and thought as a child.' That is certainly true in the story of Lucy and the wizard. Edith Nesbit did not, in fact, start writing until after the failure of her husband's business and the birth of her first child, in order to make some money. Her early stories were based on her own childhood experiences and she became immediately popular with the series of tales about the Bastable children, *The Story of the Treasure-*

Seekers (1899), *The Phoenix and the Carpet* (1904) and *The Story of the Amulet* (1906). *The Railway Children,* published in 1906, has also become a classic and adapted for films and television.

At this same time, Nesbit began writing short stories of fantasy and today she is acknowledged as the first author to tell them in a knowledgeable, not-too-serious and often humorous style. Indeed, it soon became obvious that she had learned a lot about magic in books such as *The Enchanted Castle* (1907), *The Magic City* (1910) and *The Magic World* (1912) in which normal, everyday children are the heroes. Wizards also pop up in several of her short stories— for example, the amiable Henry Birkbeck, 'Magician to the Institute of Antioch' who 'does things with eggs' in 'The Blue Mountain' and the more sinister Prince Negretti in 'The Plush Usurper' whose 'black or coloured magic won't wash clothes'. But Professor de Lara is my favourite and for those who like him, he also appears in 'Fortunatus Rex & Co' in *Nine Unlucky Tales* (1929).

SCHOOL FOR THE UNSPEAKABLE

Manly Wade Wellman

Bart is travelling by train to his new school. He is about to become a pupil at the famous old American school at Carrington and, not surprisingly, he's a bit apprehensive. His journey from the city where he lives into the countryside has given him lots of time to think about what lies ahead—and all sorts of worrying thoughts are running through his imagination. It's almost dark when Bart sets out from the station to walk to the school and he's suddenly startled when a young man with a pale face and intense, dark eyes steps out of the shadows and offers to show him the way. The boy Hoag turns out to be another pupil at the school, but his clammy handshake and the eerie things he says about what goes on there are merely hints of the terrible dark forces that await Bart at Carrington . . .

*   *   *

Bart Setwick dropped off the train at Carrington and stood for a moment on the station platform, an honest-faced, well-knit lad in tweeds. This little town and its famous school would be his home for the next eight months; but which way to the school? The sun had set, and he could barely see the shop signs across Carrington's modest main street. He hesitated, and a soft voice spoke at his very elbow:

'Are you for the school?'

Startled, Bart Setwick wheeled. In the grey twilight stood another youth, smiling thinly and waiting as if for an answer. The stranger was all of nineteen years old—that meant maturity to young Setwick, who was fifteen—and his pale face had shrewd lines to it. His tall, shambling body was clad in high-necked jersey and unfashionably tight trousers. Bart Setwick skimmed him with the quick, appraising eye of young America.

'I just got here,' he replied. 'My name's Setwick.'

'Mine's Hoag.' Out came a slender hand. Setwick took it and found it froggy-cold, with a suggestion of steel-wire muscles. 'Glad to meet you. I came down on the chance someone would drop off the train. Let me give you a lift to the school.'

Hoak turned away, felinely light for all his ungainliness, and led his new acquaintance around the corner of the little wooden railway station. Behind the structure, half hidden in its shadow, stood a shabby buggy with a lean bay horse in the shafts.

'Get in,' invited Hoag, but Bart Setwick paused for a moment. His generation was not used to such vehicles. Hoag chuckled and said, 'Oh, this is only a school wrinkle. We run to funny customs. Get in.'

Setwick obeyed. 'How about my trunk?'

'Leave it.' The taller youth swung himself in beside Setwick and took the reins. 'You'll not need it tonight.'

He snapped his tongue and the bay horse stirred,

drew them around and off down a bush-lined road. Its hoofbeats were oddly muffled.

They turned a corner, another, and came into open country. The lights of Carrington, newly kindled against the night, hung behind like a constellation settled down to Earth. Setwick felt a hint of chill that did not seem to fit the September evening.

'How far is the school from town?' he asked.

'Four or five miles,' Hoag replied in his hushed voice. 'That was deliberate on the part of the founders—they wanted to make it hard for the students to get to town for larks. It forced us to dig up our own amusements.' The pale face creased in a faint smile, as if this were a pleasantry. 'There's just a few of the right sort on hand tonight. By the way, what did you get sent out for?'

Setwick frowned his mystification. 'Why, to go to school. Dad sent me.'

'But what for? Don't you know that this is a high-class prison prep? Half of us are lunkheads that need poking along, the other half are fellows who got in scandals somewhere else. Like me.' Again Hoag smiled.

Setwick began to dislike his companion. They rolled a mile or so in silence before Hoag again asked a question:

'Do you go to church, Setwick?'

The new boy was afraid to appear priggish, and made a careless show with, 'Not very often.'

'Can you recite anything from the Bible,' Hoag's soft voice took on an anxious tinge.

'Not that I know of.'

'Good,' was the almost hearty response. 'As I was

saying, there's only a few of us at the school tonight—
only three, to be exact. And we don't like Bible-
quoters.'

Setwick laughed, trying to appear sage and cynical.
'Isn't Satan reputed to quote the Bible to his own—'

'What do you know about Satan?' interrupted
Hoag. He turned full on Setwick, studying him with
intent, dark eyes. Then, as if answering his own question: 'Little enough, I'll bet. Would you like to know
about him?'

'Sure I would,' replied Setwick, wondering what
the joke would be.

'I'll teach you after a while,' Hoag promised cryp-
tically, and silence fell again.

Half a moon was well up as they came in sight of a
dark jumble of buildings.

'Here we are,' announced Hoag, and then, throwing back his head, he emitted a wild, wordless howl
that made Setwick almost jump out of the buggy.
'That's to let the others know we're coming,' he
explained. 'Listen!'

Back came a seeming echo of the howl, shrill, faint
and eerie. The horse wavered in its muffled trot, and
Hoag clucked it back into step. They turned in at a
driveway well grown up in weeds, and two minutes
more brought them up to the rear of the closest
building. It was dim grey in the wash of moonbeams,
with blank inky rectangles for windows. Nowhere was
there a light, but as the buggy came to a halt Setwick
saw a young head pop out of a window on the lower
floor.

'Here already, Hoag?' came a high, reedy voice.

'Yes,' answered the youth at the reins, 'and I've brought a new man with me.'

Thrilling a bit to hear himself called a man, Setwick alighted.

'His name's Setwick,' went on Hoag. 'Meet Andoff, Setwick. A great friend of mine.'

Andoff flourished a hand in greeting and scrambled out over the window-sill. He was chubby and squat and even paler than Hoag, with a low forehead beneath lank, wet-looking hair, and black eyes set wide apart in a fat, stupid-looking face. His shabby jacket was too tight for him, and beneath worn trousers his legs and feet were bare. He might have been an overgrown thirteen or an undeveloped eighteen.

'Felcher ought to be along in half a second,' he volunteered.

'Entertain Setwick while I put up the buggy,' Hoag directed him.

Andoff nodded, and Hoag gathered the lines in his hands, but paused for a final word.

'No funny business yet, Andoff,' he cautioned seriously. 'Setwick, don't let this lard-bladder rag you or tell you wild stories until I come back.'

Andoff laughed shrilly. 'No, no wild stories,' he promised. 'You'll do the talking, Hoag.'

The buggy trundled away, and Andoff swung his fat, grinning face to the new arrival.

'Here comes Felcher,' he announced. 'Felcher, meet Setwick.'

Another boy had bobbed up, it seemed, from nowhere. Setwick had not seen him come around the corner of the building, or slip out of a door or window. He was probably as old as Hoag, or older, but so small as to be almost a dwarf, and frail to boot. His most notable characteristic was his hairiness. A great mop covered his head, brushed over his neck and ears, and hung unkemptly to his bright, deepset eyes. His lips and cheeks were spread with a rank down, and a curly thatch peeped through the unbuttoned collar of his soiled white shirt. The hand he offered Setwick was almost simian in its shagginess and in the hardness of its palm. Too, it was cold and damp. Setwick remembered the same thing of Hoag's handclasp.

'We're the only ones here so far,' Felcher remarked. His voice, surprisingly deep and strong for so small a creature, rang like a great bell.

'Isn't even the headmaster here?' inquired Setwick, and at that the other two began to laugh uproariously, Andoff's fife-squeal rendering an obligato to Felcher's bell-boom. Hoag, returning, asked what the fun was.

'Setwick asks,' groaned Felcher, 'why the headmaster isn't here to welcome him.'

More fife-laughter and bell-laughter.

'I doubt if Setwick would think the answer was funny,' Hoag commented, and then chuckled softly himself.

Setwick, who had been well brought up, began to grow nettled.

'Tell me about it,' he urged, in what he hoped was a bleak tone, 'and I'll join your chorus of mirth.'

Felcher and Andoff gazed at him with eyes strangely eager and learning. Then they faced Hoag.

'Let's tell him,' they both said at once, but Hoag shook his head.

'Not yet. One thing at a time. Let's have the song first.'

They began to sing. The first verse of their offering was obscene, with no pretense of humour to redeem it. Setwick had never been squeamish, but he found himself definitely repelled. The second verse seemed less objectionable, but it hardly made sense:

> *All they tried to teach here*
> *Now goes untaught.*
> *Ready, steady, each here,*
> *Knowledge we sought.*
> *What they called disaster*
> *Killed us not, O master!*
> *Rule us, we beseech here,*
> *Eye, hand and thought.*

It was something like a hymn, Setwick decided; but before what altar would such hymns be sung? Hoag must have read that question in his mind.

'You mentioned Satan in the buggy on the way out,' he recalled, his knowing face hanging like a mask in the half-dimness close to Setwick. 'Well, that was a Satanist song.'

'It was? Who made it?'

'I did,' Hoag informed him. 'How do you like it?'

Setwick made no answer. He tried to sense mockery in Hoag's voice, but could not find it. 'What,' he asked finally, 'does all this Satanist singing have to do with the headmaster?'

'A lot,' came back Felcher deeply, and 'A lot,' squealed Andoff.

Hoag gazed from one of his friends to the others,

and for the first time he smiled broadly. It gave him a toothy look.

'I believe,' he ventured quietly but weightily, 'that we might as well let Setwick in on the secret of our little circle.'

Here it would begin, the new boy decided—the school hazing of which he had heard and read so much. He had anticipated such things with something of excitement, even eagerness, but now he wanted none of them. He did not like his three companions, and he did not like the way they approached whatever it was they intended to do. He moved backward a pace or two, as if to retreat.

Swift as darting birds, Hoag and Andoff closed in at either elbow. Their chill hands clutched him and suddenly he felt light-headed and sick. Things that had been clear in the moonlight went hazy and distorted.

'Come on and sit down, Setwick,' invited Hoag, as though from a great distance. His voice did not grow loud or harsh, but it embodied real menace. 'Sit on that window-sill. Or would you like us to carry you?'

At the moment Setwick wanted only to be free of their touch, and so he walked unresistingly to the sill and scrambled up on it. Behind him was the blackness of an unknown chamber, and at his knees gathered the three who seemed so eager to tell him their private joke.

'The headmaster was a proper churchgoer,' began Hoag, as though he were the spokesman for the group. 'He didn't have any use for devils or devil-worship. Went on record against them when he addressed us in chapel. That was what started us.'

'Right,' nodded Andoff, turning up his fat, larval

face. 'Anything he outlawed, we wanted to do. Isn't that logic?'

'Logic and reason,' wound up Felcher. His hairy right hand twiddled on the sill near Setwick's thigh. In the moonlight it looked like a big, nervous spider.

Hoag resumed. 'I don't know of any prohibition of his it was easier or more fun to break.'

Setwick found that his mouth had gone dry. His tongue could barely moisten his lips. 'You mean,' he said, 'that you began to worship devils?'

Hoag nodded happily, like a teacher at an apt pupil. 'One vacation I got a book on the cult. The three of us studied it, then began ceremonies. We learned the charms and spells, forward and backward—'

'They're twice as good backward,' put in Felcher, and Andoff giggled.

'Have you any idea, Setwick.' Hoag almost cooed, 'what it was that appeared in our study the first time we burned wine and sulphur, with the proper words spoken over them?'

Setwick did not want to know. He clenched his teeth. 'If you're trying to scare me,' he managed to growl out, 'it certainly isn't going to work.'

All three laughed once more, and began to chatter out their protestations of good faith.

'I swear that we're telling the truth, Setwick.' Hoag assured him. 'Do you want to hear it, or don't you?'

Setwick had very little choice in the matter, and he realised it. 'Oh, go ahead,' he capitulated, wondering how it would do to crawl backward from the sill into the darkness of the room.

Hoag, leaned toward him, with the air as of one

confiding. 'The headmaster caught us. Caught us red-handed.'

'Book open, fire burning,' chanted Felcher.

'He had something very fine to say about the vengeance of heaven,' Hoag went on. 'We got to laughing at him. He worked up a frenzy. Finally he tried to take heaven's vengeance into his own hands—tried to visit it on us, in a very primitive way. But it didn't work.'

Andoff was laughing immoderately, his fat arms across his bent belly.

'He thought it worked,' he supplemented between high gurgles, 'but it didn't.'

'Nobody could kill us,' Felcher added. 'Not after the oaths we'd taken, and the promises that had been made us.'

'What promises?' demanded Setwick, who was struggling hard not to believe. 'Who made you any promises?'

'Those we worshipped,' Felcher told him. If he was simulating earnestness, it was a supreme bit of acting. Setwick, realising this, was more daunted than he cared to show.

'When did all these things happen?' was his next question.

'When?' echoed Hoag. 'Oh, years and years ago.'

'Years and years ago,' repeated Andoff.

'Long before you were born,' Felcher assured him.

They were standing close together, their backs to the moon that shone in Setwick's face. He could not see their expressions clearly. But their three voices—Hoag's soft, Felcher's deep and vibrant, Andoff's high and squeaky—were absolutely serious.

'I know what you're arguing within yourself,' Hoag announced somewhat smugly. 'How can we, who talk about those many past years, seem so young? That calls for an explanation, I'll admit.' He paused, as if choosing words. 'Time—for us—stands still. It came to a halt on that very night, Setwick; the night our headmaster tried to put an end to our worship.'

'And to us.' smirked the gross-bodied Andoff, with his usual air of self-congratulation at capping one of Hoag's statements.

'The worship goes on,' pronounced Felcher, in the same chanting manner that he had affected once before. 'The worship goes on, and we go on, too.'

'Which brings us to the point,' Hoag came in briskly. 'Do you want to throw in with us, Setwick?—make the fourth of this lively little party?'

'No, I don't,' snapped Setwick vehemently.

They fell silent, and gave back a little—a trio of bizarre silhouettes against the pale moonglow. Setwick could see the flash of their staring eyes among the shadows of their faces. He knew that he was afraid, but hid his fear. Pluckily he dropped from the sill to the ground. Dew from the grass spattered his sock-clad ankles between oxfords and trouser-cuffs.

'I guess it's my turn to talk,' he told them levelly. 'I'll make it short I don't like you, nor anything you've said. And I'm getting out of here.'

'We won't let you,' said Hoag, hushed but emphatic.

'We won't let you,' murmured Andoff and Felcher together, as though they had rehearsed it a thousand times.

Setwick clenched his fists. His father had taught

him to box. He took a quick, smooth stride toward Hoag and hit him hard in the face. Next moment all three had flung themselves upon him. They did not seem to strike or grapple or tug, but he went down under their assault. The shoulders of his tweed coat wallowed in sand, and he smelled crushed weeds. Hoag, on top of him, pinioned his arms with a knee on each bicep. Felcher and Andoff were stooping close.

Glaring up in helpless rage, Setwick knew once and for all that this was no schoolboy prank Never did practical jokers gather around their victim with such staring, green-gleaming eyes, such drawn jowls, such quivering lips.

Hoag bared white fangs. His pointed tongue quested once over them.

'Knife!' he muttered, and Felcher fumbled in a pocket, then passed him something that sparkled in the moonlight.

Hoag's lean hand reached for it, then whipped back. Hoag had lifted his eyes to something beyond the huddle. He choked and whimpered inarticulately, sprang up from Setwick's labouring chest, and fell back in awkward haste. The others followed his shocked stare, then as suddenly cowered and retreated in turn.

'It's the master!' wailed Andoff.

'Yes,' roared a gruff new voice. 'Your old head-master—and I've come back to master *you!*'

Rising upon one elbow, the prostrate Setwick saw what they had seen—a tall, thick-bodied figure in a long dark coat, topped with a square, distorted face and a tousle of white locks. Its eyes glittered with their own pale, hard light. As it advanced slowly and heavily it emitted a snigger of murderous joy. Even at first glance Setwick was aware that it cast no shadow.

'I am in time,' mouthed the newcomer. 'You were going to kill this poor boy.'

Hoag had recovered and made a stand. 'Kill him?' he quavered, seeming to fawn before the threatening presence. 'No. We'd have given him life—'

'You call it life!' trumpeted the long-coated one. 'You'd have sucked out his blood to teem your own dead veins, damned him to your filthy condition. But I'm here to prevent you!'

A finger pointed, huge and knuckly, and then came a torrent of language. To the nerve-stunned Setwick it sounded like a bit from the New Testament, or perhaps from the Book of Common Prayer. All at once he remembered Hoag's avowed dislike for such quotations.

His three erstwhile assailants reeled as if before a high wind that chilled or scorched. 'No, no! Don't!' they begged wretchedly.

The square old face gaped open and spewed merciless laughter. The knuckly finger traced a cross in the air, and the trio wailed in chorus as though the sign had been drawn upon their flesh with a tongue of flame.

Hoag dropped to his knees. 'Don't!' he sobbed.

'I have power,' mocked their tormentor. 'During years shut up I won it, and now I'll use it.' Again a triumphant burst of mirth. 'I know you're damned and can't be killed, but you can be tortured! I'll make you crawl like worms before I'm done with you!'

Setwick gained his shaky feet. The long coat and the blocky head leaned toward him.

'Run, you!' dinned a rough roar in his ears. 'Get out of here—and thank God for the chance!'

Setwick ran, staggering. He blundered through the weeds of the driveway, gained the road beyond. In the distance gleamed the lights of Carrington. As he turned his face toward them and quickened his pace he began to weep, chokingly, hysterically, exhaustingly.

He did not stop running until he reached the platform in front of the station. A clock across the street struck ten, in a deep voice not unlike Felcher's. Setwick breathed deeply, fished out his handkerchief and mopped his face. His hand was quivering like a grass stalk in a breeze.

'Beg pardon!' came a cheery hail. 'You must be Setwick.'

As once before on this same platform, he whirled around with startled speed. Within touch of him stood a broad-shouldered man of thirty or so, with hornrimmed spectacles. He wore a neat Norfolk jacket and flannels. A short briar pipe was clamped in a good-humoured mouth.

'I'm Collins, one of the masters at the school,' he introduced himself. 'If you're Setwick, you've had us worried. We expected you on that seven o'clock train-you know. I dropped down to see if I couldn't trace you.'

Setwick found a little of his lost wind. 'But I've—been to the school,' he mumbled protestingly. His hand, still trembling, gestured vaguely along the way he had come.

Collins threw back his head and laughed, then apologised.

'Sorry,' he said. 'It's no joke if you really had all that walk for nothing. Why, that old place is deserted—used to be a catch-all for incorrigible rich boys. They closed it about fifty years ago, when the headmaster went mad and killed three of his pupils. As a matter of coincidence, the master himself died just this afternoon, in the state hospital for the insane.'

*   *   *

MANLY WADE WELLMAN is famous for having written some of the best supernatural stories set in rural American locations. His knowledge of the folk traditions of the backwoods areas of the US give all his tales a really authentic atmosphere and it is more than possible that creepy Carrington School is based on just such a place in the wilds of North Carolina where the author lived and worked for many years. Although Manly Wade Wellman was born in Africa, where his father was a medical officer, he went to an American college before becoming a newspaper reporter. His fascination with the supernatural led to him writing his first stories for the famous horror magazine, *Weird Tales*, and these became very popular with readers. He devised a series of stories for the publication featuring John Thurnstone, an occult detective, including the classic, *The School of Darkness* (1985) which is also about a school you would have to be very brave to attend. It, too, had a terrifying headmaster not unlike the one you will meet in the next story.

THE DEMON HEADMASTER

Gillian Cross

No one knows what his name is—they just call him 'The Headmaster'. But there is no avoiding those huge, green eyes when he takes off his dark glasses and hypnotises anyone who disobeys him. Nor shivering when he speaks his famous line to either children or adults, 'I hope you are not going to be a person who won't cooperate with me!' The Demon Headmaster rules his school—which is not usually named, although it has been referred to as St Campions—with a sinister power as he plots to take over the world. He's a modern version of the 'Mad Professor'. In fact, all that stands between him and his plans is a smart group of pupils who have formed an organisation known as SPLAT—the Society for the Protection of our Lives Against Them. In the list of teachers with magic powers, The Demon Headmaster belongs near the top and in this story, the man with the evil green eyes sets about using his power to put a stop to one of his pet hates—people having fun . . .

* * *

The tall man from across the road was outside Bernadine's house, looking at the notice in the window.

```
┌─────────────────────────────────────────┐
│                                           │
│        FINAL CARNIVAL MEETING             │
│                                           │
│               HERE!!!                     │
│                                           │
│          TONIGHT AT 7:30 PM               │
│                                           │
│             ALL WELCOME                   │
│                                           │
│        IF YOU CARE—BE THERE!!!            │
│                                           │
└─────────────────────────────────────────┘
```

'I'm going to be the firebird!' Bernadine said. She was so excited that she kept telling people.

The man scowled through his dark glasses. 'Carnivals are noisy and disorderly.'

Bernadine pulled a face at him and dodged past, heading for her back door. The meeting was about to start and the kitchen was crammed with people. Bernadine's mother was waving her cassette recorder above her head.

'I'm taping you all! So I know who's promised what!'

Everyone laughed. As she switched it on, the back door opened. In stalked the man in dark glasses. Why had he come? Bernadine stared at him.

'Manners!' her mother hissed.

Her father nudged her. 'Don't gawp. Go round to Stevie's and fetch your costume.'

The firebird costume! Forgetting the man in dark glasses, Bernadine slipped through the back door. As she closed it behind her, all the noise in the kitchen stopped. Which was odd, because Carnival meetings were never quiet. She peered through the glass, to see what was happening.

Everyone in the kitchen was very still, gazing at the tall man. Slowly, he took off his dark glasses. His eyes were strange. Sea green and luminous.

'You are all very tired,' he murmured—and suddenly everyone started yawning. *Weird*, Bernadine thought. She would have stayed to see what happened, but she couldn't wait. She wanted to be at her cousin Stevie's house, trying on the firebird costume. Who cared about Dark Glasses?

When she came back, the house was silent. She opened the back door and found the kitchen was empty, except for her parents.

'What's up?' she said. 'Did the Carnival meeting finish early?'

'There will not be a Carnival,' her mother said, in a dull, flat voice.

'*What?*'

Her father nodded. 'No bands. No processions. No dancing in the street.' His voice was the same. 'Carnivals are unimportant and wasteful.'

Bernadine stared. 'No Carnival?'

'There will not be a Carnival,' her parents said together. 'No bands. No processions. No dancing in the street. Carnivals are unimportant and wasteful.'

That was all they would say. The same words, over and over again. Bernadine went to bed, but she was too miserable to sleep.

At one o'clock in the morning, she suddenly remembered the cassette recorder. Slipping out of bed, she crept into the kitchen and found it. When she'd rewound the tape, she turned the volume down and pressed PLAY.

Faintly, she heard laughing and joking. Then an abrupt silence. Then the voice of the man in dark glasses.

You are all very tired . . .

What was he up to?

Suddenly, his voice changed. *You will all do what I say,* he snapped. *Do you understand?*

We understand. Everyone who answered sounded dull and mechanical—like Bernadine's parents. She shuddered.

There will not be a Carnival, the tall man said. *No bands. No fancy dress. No processions. No dancing in the street. Carnivals are unimportant and wasteful.*

The mechanical voices repeated his words.

Bernadine sat down, feeling weak. She knew now what had happened. He'd hypnotised them, to stop the Carnival.

But what was she going to do?

She sat and thought, for an hour. By the time she went back to bed, she had a plan.

Next day, at school, everyone was miserable.

'*There will not be a Carnival,*' Stevie growled. 'That's all my dad would say.'

His friend Nathan nodded. '*No dancing in the street. Carnivals are unimportant and wasteful.*'

Stevie sighed. 'Looks as if you'll miss out on being the firebird, Bernie.'

'No, I won't!' Bernadine tossed her head. 'We can get the Carnival ready without our parents. We know what we have to do!'

'We can decorate the lorries,' Nathan said. 'And set up the loudspeakers. But we can't drive, or play the music.'

Bernadine smiled, mysteriously. 'Leave that to Stevie and me.' She beckoned Stevie away from everyone else. 'Think you can edit this?' she murmured . . .

And she took out the tape.

On Carnival Day, Bernadine pulled on the firebird costume and ran downstairs.

Her father frowned. 'There will not be a Carnival—'

'Yes, there will,' Bernadine said.

Dodging her mother, who tried to grab her, she slipped outside. All along the street, other children in fancy dress were dodging their parents too. Bernadine waved across the road, signalling to Stevie. He started his tape and Bernadine's voice boomed from the loudspeakers.

'CARNIVAL!'

She looked across the street, at the tall man's house. *Come on!* she thought.

CARNIVAL! boomed the tape.

An upstairs window opened across the street. The man in dark glasses looked out scornfully.

'You have wasted your time decorating those lorries,' he said. 'There will not be a Carnival.' He took off his glasses.

Stevie glanced at Bernadine, but she shook her head. *Not yet.*

The man stared down at the crowd for a moment. Then he opened his mouth. 'Listen!' he snapped.

Everyone turned to look at him, and Bernadine nodded to Stevie. *Now!*

Stevie switched on. As the man began speaking, his voice was drowned by—itself. From every loudspeaker blared the words he'd spoken at the meeting. Edited by Stevie.

THERE WILL . . . BE A CARNIVAL . . . BANDS . . . FANCY DRESS . . . PROCESSIONS . . . DANCING IN THE STREET.

The man glared at Bernadine. She could see he was speaking louder, but it was no use. The deafening loudspeakers went on trumpeting his voice.

CARNIVALS ARE . . . IMPORTANT.

All along the street, grown-ups were fetching out their Carnival costumes. Or starting up lorries. Or seizing musical instruments.

THERE WILL . . . BE A CARNIVAL . . .

With a blare of brass and an explosion of dancing, the Carnival procession set off. The tall man slammed his window shut, in disgust, and Bernadine grinned. Then she danced off after the band.

The most joyful firebird the Carnival had ever seen.

*   *   *

GILLIAN CROSS actually worked in a school so she knows all about the way pupils and teachers interact in and out of the classroom. Which is just one of the reasons why her series of books about The Demon Headmaster have become so popular and also been turned into a television series and a musical play. Gillian studied at Oxford University and was a child-minder and an assistant to an MP before the awards starting coming in for the books she was writing in her spare time. The idea for the wicked headmaster actually came from Gillian's daughter, Elizabeth, and at one time the author planned to make one of the members of SPLAT, Harvey, a shape-shifter who could transform himself into objects like teapots or a tape-recorder. The success of the books, including *The Prime Minister's Brain* (1985). *The Demon Headmaster Strikes Again* (1996) and *The Demon Headmaster Takes Over* (1997) is also due to her ability to mix fantasy and reality and show that it is possible to outwit really evil forces . . . whatever your age.

GHOSTCLUSTERS

Humphrey Carpenter

Walpurgis Night is no ordinary night and Mr Majeika is no ordinary wizard. It is the evening of 1 May when, according to tradition, wizards and witches meet for a big celebration. The Harz Mountains in Germany are said to be the most famous spot in the world for this annual get-together with magic-makers flying in from all over the place on their broomsticks. Mr Majeika is a wizard who has not yet completed his Sorcery Exams and, as a result, has to earn his living at St Barty's School where he is Class Three's form teacher. The kids in his class love him—especially Thomas Grey and his friend Melanie Brace-Girdle, the only ones to know his secret—the one exception being the nasty Hamish Bigmore. Tom and Melanie are a bit like Harry Potter and the redoubtable Hermione Granger and they reckon anyone who can magic up a plate of chips or turn someone into a frog must have as much wizardry at his fingertips as Professor Snape at Hogwarts. (J. K. Rowling has, incidentally, said that Hallowe'en is her favourite night and Professor Snape was based on one of her own teachers—though she's not saying who!) In this story, the head of St Barty's, Mr Potter, has decided to have a school outing to Chutney Castle—on Walpurgis Night. And with Mr Majeika along for the ride, the magic—and the surprises—come thick and fast . . .

*   *   *

Poor Mr Majeika. It was his first Walpurgis Night away from Walpurgis and he knew he would have to celebrate it all by himself. Walpurgis Night was the biggest night of the year, up there in the land in the sky where the Wizards and the Witches come from, and every Walpurgian always tried to be back home that night, so that they wouldn't miss the marvellous celebrations—the dancing around the Everlasting Bonfire, the Marrowbone and Bromide Supper, and most of all the unforgettable sight of the Witches' Knitting Circle performing the Dance of the Seven Cobwebs. But poor Mr Majeika! There was no way that *he* could get back to Walpurgis for this year's festivities. He had been banished to Britland, and there he must stay, as a teacher, until he had proved himself worthy to return home and complete his Sorcery Exams.

'Poor Majeika!' mused the Worshipful Wizard, as he contemplated the plight of the little chap down there in Britland. 'Poor Majeika! Walpurgis Night, and he'll be all by himself.'

'Poor me,' Mr Majeika was thinking, down there at his windmill. 'Walpurgis Night and I'll be all by myself.' But he had decided to organize his own Walpurgis celebrations, and pretend he was back in Walpurgis with all the other Wizards and Witches. He had built an enormous bonfire, piling it high with oddly named wild flowers and strange weeds from the hedgerows, and he had made himself a crown of bogweed, just like everyone would be wearing up there in Walpurgis. That night, when he got back from school, he would light it and dance round it in the moonlight, chanting Walpurgian chants.

He couldn't wait!

'Ah, Majeika,' said Mr Potter, when Mr Majeika rolled up at St Barty's School that morning on his trike, 'it's a very special day today, isn't it?'

'Yes, yes, Mr Potter,' said Mr Majeika eagerly, 'but how did you know?' For a moment, he wondered whether Walpurgis Night was celebrated in Much Barty. How exciting that would be! He could imagine Mrs Brace-Girdle and the village ladies dancing round a bonfire; they'd look almost as remarkable as the Witches' Knitting Circle.

'How did I know, Majeika?' asked Mr Potter, puzzled. 'Why, because I organized the whole thing myself.'

'Organized it, Mr Potter?'

'Yes, yes, Majeika—the annual School Outing. You haven't forgotten, Majeika, have you? We're going on our annual school trip and this year the destination is Chutney Castle.'

'Really, Mr Potter?' said Mr Majeika. 'That sounds exciting.' Not quite as exciting as Walpurgis Night, perhaps, but still pretty good. He had never seen a Britland castle, though he had visited several in distant parts of Walpurgis, most of them occupied by rather dangerous giants and ogres.

'Chutney Castle,' said Mr Potter impressively, 'has been standing, Majeika, since the tenth century.'

'Has it really!' said Mr Majeika. 'Wouldn't it rather sit down?'

*

'Poor Majeika,' said the Worshipful Wizard yet again. And this time he was saying it out loud to one of the Senior Wizards, Wizard Thymes. 'If there was only some way we could keep him in touch with our Walpurgis Night celebrations up here . . .'

Wizard Thymes scratched his head with the end of his wand. 'Hmm,' he said thoughtfully. 'Perhaps if one of us were to go down and visit him?'

The Worshipful Wizard gave a shudder. 'Well, not one of *us*,' he said firmly. 'I've been already, and it was awful.' He was remembering the thorn bushes, and all the wind on the way down.

'Possibly,' said Wizard Thymes, 'some junior Walpurgian, someone who would be willing to get a little fresh air and see the wide world?'

A big coach was parked outside St Barty's School, with the words *Jolly Jasper's Merrie Medieval Tours* painted on the side. 'All set, everyone?' called Mr Potter. 'The bus will take us to the station, where as a special treat we shall be going by steam train to Chutney Junction, where another bus will pick us up and deliver us to Chutney Castle. All aboard, everyone!'

'Can't go yet,' said the driver. 'Jolly Jasper, the boss, hasn't turned up.'

'But it's already ten o'clock,' said Mr Potter anxiously. 'At this rate the children will miss the delicious lunch that has been arranged for them at Chutney Castle.'

'I'll tell you what,' said Councillor Mrs Brace-Girdle, who had come to see her daughter Melanie off, 'I'll wait here for this Jolly Jasper person and bring him on by car. No reason why he should spoil your day.'

'That's very good of you, Bunty,' said Mr Potter. 'Mrs Brace-Girdle to the rescue, as usual. Off we go, everyone! Next stop, the station.'

'Station?' asked Mr Majeika. 'What's a station?'

The Worshipful Wizard had called a meeting of all the Walpurgians. He made a little speech about how lonely Majeika would be. 'So,' he concluded, 'who would like to pop down there, just for a day and a night, and make Apprentice Wizard Majeika a really happy Walpurgian, by celebrating Walpurgis Night with him?'

No one put their hand up. (Wilhelmina Worlock had gone on a day trip to the back of the moon and so was not there to volunteer.)

'Hm,' said the Worshipful Wizard. 'I see, no volunteers.' He turned to Wizard Thymes. 'That makes things a little difficult.'

Wizard Thymes scratched his head once again. 'Well,' he said, 'not everyone is here, you know. There is one name I can think of. And he just *might* agree to go. If you want to see him, we'll have to go down to the Catacombs . . .'

'Well,' said Melanie to Mr Majeika, 'now you know what a station looks like.' They were standing on the platform, waiting for the special steam train.

'Yes,' said Mr Majeika doubtfully, looking around him. 'But I still don't know what it's for.'

'I'll explain,' said Thomas. 'You see—'

But at that moment there was a shriek of a whistle, and they could see the steam train puffing towards them down the line.

Mr Majeika screamed in fright and took to his heels. 'A dragon! It's a dragon!'

Thomas and Melanie ran after him and caught hold of him, dragging him back out of the waiting room, where he was trying to hide. 'It isn't a dragon,' said Melanie firmly. 'It's just a train.'

The train pulled in, and the engine steamed past them, with its fire roaring in the cab. Mr Majeika was shaking all over with fright. 'Look! Fire, fire! And steam and smoke!' he cried. 'Only dragons breathe steam and smoke and have fires in their bellies like that.'

'Ah, there you are, Majeika,' said Mr Potter, strolling down the platform. 'In you get.'

'I'm not riding on a dragon, Mr Potter,' quivered Mr Majeika.

'Oh yes you are,' said Melanie firmly. 'All aboard, Mr Majeika!'

The Walpurgian Catacombs are the darkest, ghostliest and ghastliest place in all Walpurgis, hung with cobwebs and lit with a sinister greenish light. Even the Worshipful Wizard was a little nervous as he and Wizard Thymes groped their way down a narrow passage.

'Are you sure this is the right place, Thymes?' asked the Worshipful Wizard anxiously. 'I wouldn't want to take a wrong turning—you never know what you might meet.'

'No indeed,' said Wizard Thymes. 'But this should be the right chamber. If I remember, he lives in a glass coffin in here.' He ducked under a narrow archway and led the Worshipful Wizard into a particularly eerie-looking cave.

'A glass coffin?' asked the Worshipful Wizard. 'Did you say coffin?'

'Well, well, isn't this exciting, children?' said Mr Potter, surveying the chaos around him in the train.

Fighting had broken out among Class Three the moment the whistle had blown and the train set off from Much Barty. Several of them had got into the luggage rack and the rest of them were quarrelling about who could have seats next to the windows.

'Ah, Majeika,' said Mr Potter, seeing Mr Majeika tottering nervously down the corridor, 'you can take charge.' And Mr Potter went and shut himself in the toilet.

'T-take ch-charge, Mr Potter?' said Mr Majeika nervously, peering out of the corridor window. 'J-just as you say. But shouldn't someone keep an eye on that dragon? It's still breathing fire, you know.'

Thomas and Melanie, looking for seats, found an empty compartment. Empty, that is, save for Hamish Bigmore, who was sitting there all by himself, sprinkling salt on to a bag of crisps.

'Mind if we join you, Hamish?' asked Melanie.

'Most certainly I mind,' said Hamish Bigmore. 'I've got my dad's season ticket, and he always travels First Class. Get out, before I call the guard!' And he pointed at the *First Class Ticket Holders Only* sign on the window.

Wizard Thymes had found the glass coffin, and was knocking on it. 'Come out, come out, whoever you are!' he intoned.

The glass was dirty, and the Worshipful Wizard

couldn't see who, or what, was inside the coffin. 'Are you sure this is a good idea?' he asked anxiously.

It's the proper spell to raise them, you know,' said Wizard Thymes. And he intoned again: 'Come out, come out, whoever you are!'

The glass coffin began to creak open.

Mr Majeika was beginning to get used to the fact that they were travelling by dragon. After all, the dreadful creature hadn't eaten them yet. But he could imagine what it would be like if it did. A big mouth would open and suddenly everything would go dark as you were popped into the dragon's tummy.

At that moment everything went dark.

Mr Majeika screamed.

'It's all right, Mr Majeika!' called Melanie.

'The dragon's swallowed us up!' yelled Mr Majeika.

'No it hasn't,' said Thomas soothingly. 'We're just in a tunnel, that's all.'

Mr Potter emerged from the toilet. 'Ah, Majeika,' he said, 'you look as if you're enjoying yourself. Nothing like a nice relaxing day out, is there?'

'No, Mr Potter,' quivered Mr Majeika.

'Come out, come out, whoever you are!' intoned Wizard Thymes yet again, and lit up the end of his wand so that the greenish light in the cave became a little stronger.

'Go away,' said a little voice from the crack where the coffin had opened. 'I don't like the light. It makes me nervous.'

'Come out, come out, whoever you are!' repeated Wizard Thymes.

'Shan't,' said the little voice.

'Oh, yes, you will,' said Wizard Thymes firmly, putting his hand in the crack. 'Out you come!'

And out, very unwillingly, came a thin shivering little ghost with long grey hair and a face as white as a sheet.

'This,' said Wizard Thymes to the Worshipful Wizard, 'is Phil Spectre.'

The pale little face stared up at them.

'Phil Spectre,' announced the Worshipful Wizard, 'you have been chosen to visit Britland.'

'Please, no!' shivered the ghost, trying to get back into the glass coffin. But Wizard Thymes got hold of him by the neck.

'It's an order,' he told the ghost.

'No!' shrieked the ghost, wriggling so hard that his head fell off. 'It always does that when I'm frightened,' he explained, putting it on again.

'Listen, Spectre,' said the Worshipful Wizard firmly, 'you can't spend the rest of your life—I mean death—hanging about in this miserable coffin. Get out and do the job for which you were trained! You're supposed to haunt people.'

'That's right, Spectre,' said Wizard Thymes. 'It's high time you spooked.'

'But I don't want to haunt anyone, sir,' said Phil Spectre miserably. 'I'm too—too shy. I used to do a bit of haunting, on the quiet, but I kept scaring myself to death. That's why I hide away here, sir, with nothing but a few other ghosts flitting past now and then.'

'You are a wretched little fellow, aren't you?' observed the Worshipful Wizard. 'Don't you ever get lonely?'

'Well, sir,' said Phil Spectre, 'a bit, now and then.'

'Exactly so. Well, Apprentice Wizard Majeika is *very* lonely, down there in Britland, and you have been chosen to go and cheer him up—just for the one night, Walpurgis Night.'

'But, sir—'

'I won't hear another word against it, Spectre. Off you go!' But he wouldn't. So Wizard Thymes and the Worshipful Wizard had to push poor Phil Spectre through the hole that leads from Walpurgis into the sky, and down to Britland. The poor creature screamed as he fell.

If he had been wearing a white sheet, such as ghosts often put on, it would have acted as a parachute. But he was a medieval-style ghost, since he dated from the days of Henry the Eighth, and his doublet and hose didn't act as any kind of brake against the wind. He fell very fast and landed with a bump in a field just outside Much Barty. Ghosts weigh nothing at all, so he was not hurt, but the whole thing had been a frightful shock.

'Moo!' said a cow just behind him and poor Phil Spectre would have leapt out of his skin, if he had had a skin. As it was, he gave a little scream, and the book of *Instructions for Walpurgians in the Country of the Britlanders* fell out of his pocket.

That reminded him. He was supposed to look up his orders in the book. 'Upon arrival in Much Barty,' he read, 'make yourself known immediately to Apprentice Wizard Majeika, who will usually be found at St Barty's School.'

Phil Spectre set off down the road.

*

'Right,' muttered Mrs Brace-Girdle, getting into her car and slamming the door. 'I'm off. Drat this Jolly Jasper character for not turning up and keeping me waiting for no purpose. I'm off!'

She had just put the car into gear when she saw someone in medieval costume walking down the road.

'So there you are!' snorted Mrs Brace-Girdle, winding down her window. 'A fine time to arrive, I must say. Hop in the back. The door isn't locked.'

So it wasn't, but Phil Spectre didn't need to open doors. He passed through this one and materialized on the other side, sitting himself down on the back seat of Mrs Brace-Girdle's car. There was nothing about this Britlander in his handbook, but he recognized in Mrs Brace-Girdle the look of someone who expects to be obeyed.

'Now,' said Mrs Brace-Girdle, driving off, 'we'll have you at Chutney Castle in no time.'

At Chutney Castle, the owner, Lord Reg Pickles, stared gloomily out of the window at the St Barty's School party, which was just getting out of the coach. 'Not another bloomin' school party,' muttered Lord Reg.

'Never mind, dearie,' said his wife, Lady Lillie. 'Helps to pay the bills, don't it, Reg?'

Outside, Mr Potter was explaining the history of Chutney Castle to Mr Majeika. 'The present owner is Lord Reg Pickles, the founder of Bartyshire's famous Plumptious Pickled Onions and Gourmet Gherkins, delicacies which no doubt you have often sampled, Majeika?'

'Not me, Mr Potter,' said Mr Majeika.

'And here he is, children,' called Mr Potter, seeing Lord Reg emerging from under the entrance arch. 'An actual member of the Great British Aristocracy! A real live Lord!'

'Pleased to meet you, children,' said Lord Reg, who was clutching a jar of Plumptious Pickled Onions. 'May I present my wife, the Lady Lillie?'

'All right, you lot,' called Lady Lillie. 'The Souvenir Shop is over there. Get your money out!'

The children made a stampede for souvenirs. 'My, isn't this fun, Majeika?' said Mr Potter. 'A real piece of history.'

'Yes, Mr Potter,' said Mr Majeika dutifully.

'Oh, and Majeika, would you supervise the unloading of the overnight bags?'

'Bags, Mr Potter? What sort of bags?'

'Suitcases, my dear chap. Don't say you didn't bring one? Surely you knew we were going to stay the night?'

'No, I didn't,' said Mr Majeika miserably, thinking of his Walpurgis Night bonfire, which now he would never have the chance to light.

Mrs Brace-Girdle, who was still very cross, was driving rather fast. She came round a corner and, finding that there was a red traffic light in front of her, had to brake hard. The car bumped to a halt and Phil Spectre's head fell off.

There was a policeman on duty by the traffic lights, and Mrs Brace-Girdle rolled down her window. 'Constable, can you tell me the way to Chutney Castle?'

The policeman came over and told her. The lights

changed to green, and as the car drove off the policeman turned rather green too. There had been a
person on the back seat holding his head on his lap.
And the head had turned and looked at him.

Lady Lillie Pickles was taking—or rather, dragging—
the children on a conducted tour of the castle. In
particular, she was dragging Hamish Bigmore, who
had ignored every sign that said 'Do Not Touch'.

'This way, children,' she called. 'And remember,
don't touch a thing.'

While her back was turned, Hamish picked up an
antique vase labelled 'Chinese, Ming Period'.

'My dad's got nicer stuff than that,' said Hamish.

Lady Lillie turned and saw the vase in his hand. 'I
said *don't touch*!' she snapped and smacked his hand.

Then one of the other children tripped over a rope
and her attention was distracted. Hamish dropped
the vase and it shattered into a million pieces.

'Oh, no!' breathed Thomas.

But Mr Majeika was bringing up the rear of the
file of children and he caught sight of the disaster.
In a moment he had flicked his tuft of hair and—
magically—the vase had reassembled itself and
floated up to the place on the table where it had
been sitting.

Only Thomas and Melanie spotted this. They
looked at each other.

'He's still—' said Melanie.

'—magical, Melanie,' said Thomas.

'Magnificent, isn't it, Majeika?' said Mr Potter to Mr
Majeika as they entered the Great Hall.

'Very nice, Mr Potter,' said Mr Majeika. 'But I used to live in a huge place just like this, you know.'

'You never?' said Lord Reg, impressed. 'What, you mean with a load of proper lords and ladies and all that?'

'No,' said Mr Majeika, 'with a load of proper Wizards and Witches. I mean—it was a very wizard place.'

'Oh yeah?' said Lord Reg. 'Course, we weren't a Lord and Lady from birth, you know.'

'Really?' said Mr Potter. 'You do surprise me, your lordship.'

'Nope,' said Lord Reg. 'The missus, when I first knew her, was an onion pickler in Poplar.'

'You don't say,' remarked Mr Potter. 'I'd never have guessed, would you, Majeika?'

'Certainly not, Mr Potter,' said Mr Majeika.

'Course, we're full of class now,' said Lord Reg. 'Yes, it's surprising what pickled onions can do for a man, Mr Potter.' He gave a loud burp.

'Yes?' said Mr Potter politely.

'Yup,' said Lord Reg, patting his stomach. 'I mean, once yer onions takes off, you can be a real big noise.' He burped again.

'I must say,' said Mrs Brace-Girdle, turning down the lane that was signposted *To Chutney Castle*, 'for someone who calls himself Jolly Jasper, you are remarkably silent.'

On the back seat, Phil Spectre was fitting his head on to his shoulders again. He made no reply.

'And you can leave *that* alone too,' snapped Lady Lillie, snatching Hamish Bigmore away from a medieval instrument of torture, into which he had been trying to squeeze the foot of a small boy from Class Three.

'Well, your lordship,' observed Mr Potter, looking around the dungeon, 'you've certainly got everything here.'

'Nearly everything, Mr Potter,' answered Lord Reg, opening his jar and offering Mr Potter a pickled onion. 'There is just one thing what we lack, what would be the icing on the pickle, so to speak, if we had it.'

'And what's that, Lord Pickles?' asked Mr Majeika.

'A resident Ghost,' said Lord Reg Pickles, popping an onion into his mouth.

Mrs Brace-Girdle parked her car by the castle draw-bridge and got out, banging her door shut. 'You'd better wait in there till I've told them that Jolly Jasper has arrived,' she said. 'It might be quite the wrong moment if you rushed in there now.'

She strode under the archway, up the main staircase and into the Great Hall. Lord Reg was just leading Mr Potter and Mr Majeika back from the dungeons.

'Ah, Mr Potter!' said Mrs Brace-Girdle. 'I've brought him with me. Is it all right for me to send him in straight away?'

'Who, Bunty?' asked Mr Potter, puzzled.

'Why,' said Mrs Brace-Girdle, 'Jolly Jasper, the Merrie Minstrel.'

'Jolly Jasper?' repeated Mr Potter, puzzled. 'But Jolly Jasper has been here for hours. He met us at Chutney Junction and drove the coach up here. He's down in the courtyard right now, playing his lute.'

Mrs Brace-Girdle's face fell. 'Then who have I brought in my car?'

Downstairs, by the drawbridge, Lady Lillie was looking after the combined Souvenir Shop and ticket office. She heard the turnstile creak; someone must be arriving.

'Yes?' she said. 'Adult ticket? Child or old age pensioner?'

Phil Spectre, who was rather short, picked his head off his shoulders with one hand and held it up to the ticket window.

'Ghost ticket, please,' said the head.

Lady Lillie screamed.

'Now, children!' called Mr Potter. 'It's time to go and look at the suits of armour in the Long Gallery. This is a particularly dark and sinister part of the castle, so don't forget to watch out for any ghosts!' He turned to Mr Majeika. 'Just my little joke, Majeika. I don't believe in ghosts.'

'Don't you, Mr Potter?' said Mr Majeika nervously. He knew all about ghosts from Walpurgis. They were sinister fellows who lived down in the Catacombs, where most Witches and Wizards didn't like to go at all. He'd never seen one and he didn't want to start now.

'Don't worry, Mr Majeika,' said Melanie, who could see he was nervous. 'We'll protect you from the ghosts.'

'Ghosts!' snorted Hamish Bigmore. 'Only babies believe in ghosts!'

*

Phil Spectre thought the castle looked rather nice inside—just the place to do a haunting, if you were that way inclined—but he was frightfully nervous. He kept hearing distant voices, as if there were . . . *people* about.

Some ghosts don't believe in people but Phil Spectre knew better. Down there in the Catacombs of Walpurgis, his granny ghost had told him horrifying tales about people who came in the night to frighten poor little ghosts; people who opened doors, rather than gliding through the woodwork; people who walked up and downstairs, rather than floating in the air; people who spoke words, rather than giving moans and shrieks; people who had horrible things like cameras and tape-recorders and radios, rather than a nice comforting iron ball and chain; people who were made of flesh and blood, rather than being just a wisp of ectoplasm, or a bone-rattling skeleton. 'But it's all right, my poor little ghostie,' she had told him. 'If you're lucky, you may never meet a—person!'

Now, in Chutney Castle, poor Phil Spectre knew he was *surrounded* by people. He looked for somewhere to hide.

He found a room full of suits of armour. One of those would do nicely.

'Here we are, then, children,' said Mr Potter, as they came into the armoury. 'Most of this armour dates from the days of Henry the Eighth. Isn't it magnificent?'

'Load of rusty old rubbish,' said Hamish Bigmore. 'They'd have done better to melt it all down into baked bean cans. Yah!' And he took hold of the biggest suit of armour and shook it so that it rattled noisily.

Inside, poor Phil Spectre was being shaken about dreadfully. His granny was right! People were awful. He was terrified. And he was also very angry. What right had this creature to come and frighten him like that? He'd show it!

Hamish Bigmore turned his back on the suit of armour. 'Baked beans,' he sneered. 'I'd rather have a can of baked beans. *Oucchh!*'

The suit of armour had kicked him very hard on the bottom.

Thomas and Melanie had seen it happen and were laughing till tears ran down their faces. 'It must have been a ghost, Hamish!' said Thomas.

Hamish Bigmore scowled at them. 'It just tipped over and kicked me by accident,' he said. 'Only babies believe in ghosts.'

'W-was it really a ghost?' Mr Majeika asked Thomas and Melanie, when they were back in the Great Hall.

'Search us,' said Thomas. 'But there was something in there that kicked Hamish.'

'And it certainly wasn't us,' said Melanie. 'I wouldn't be in the least surprised if, in an old castle like this, there wasn't a ghost floating about the place.'

'Oh d-dear,' said Mr Majeika.

Phil Spectre had some difficulty in getting out of the suit of armour. He wondered where it was really safe to hide. Then he remembered that he shouldn't be hiding at all. He should be looking for Mr Majeika.

How had he got carried off to this wretched castle?
He was supposed to be in Much Barty, searching for
Mr Majeika at the school.

Suddenly he heard a voice in the passage outside.
He froze; it was a *person* again—how frightening!

'Mr Majeika!' called the voice (it was Thomas).
'Mr Majeika! The rooms we're going to sleep in are
upstairs. Are you coming up to see your bedroom?'

Phil Spectre couldn't believe his ears. Mr Majeika
was here—in the castle! What a stroke of luck. Now
all he had to do was to find him and introduce himself to this fellow Walpurgian. But if only he could
manage it without running into any more *people.*

Very cautiously, he stuck his head through the door
and peeped out. Yes, the coast seemed to be clear.
Silently, he floated out and up the stairs towards the
bedrooms.

In his bedroom, Mr Majeika gave a flick of his tuft
of hair, and there stood an overnight bag containing
night-shirt, toothbrush and night-cap. 'There,' he
said, 'that should do it.'

'Gosh,' said Thomas.

'Well,' said Melanie, 'sleep well, Mr Majeika. I'm
sure there aren't any ghosts here really, and if there
are, they probably won't disturb you.'

'I hope n-not,' said Mr Majeika.

Outside, Phil Spectre was groping his way nervously
along the dark corridor. Which door should he try?

Lady Lillie Pickles was taking her teeth out for
the night when she heard her bedroom door open
behind her. 'Is that you, Reg?' she asked without

looking round. 'Make us a mug of cocoa, there's a dear. All those Gourmet Gherkins we had for supper have given me a touch of wind.'

There was no reply. Lady Lillie looked in her mirror—and saw a ghostly pale head regarding her from the doorway. She screamed.

When he had got back his nerve—the encounter with the lady who could take out her teeth (something no ghost had ever learnt to do) had thoroughly frightened him—Phil Spectre floated on down the corridor. 'Mr Majeika!' he called softly, in case the Apprentice Wizard could somehow hear him. 'Mr Majeika!'

Mr Majeika was just dropping off to sleep when he thought he heard someone calling his name. Was it Thomas or Melanie? Yawning, he got out of bed and tiptoed to the door. The whole place still frightened him. Why did they have to come to this horrible creepy castle, especially on Walpurgis Night, when he wanted to be at home, dancing round his bonfire?

He opened the door. There was no one in the corridor.

But again he heard the voice. 'Mr Majeika!' it called softly.

Shivering with cold and nerves, Mr Majeika gingerly walked to where he thought the voice came from.

'Mr Majeika!' called Phil Spectre desperately. His nerves were getting quite worn down. If he didn't find the Apprentice Wizard soon, he'd get on to Walpurgis and demand that they take him back at once.

He might even get back in time for some of the famous Walpurgis Night celebrations he had heard so much about, but had never yet attended.

There was nobody to be seen and the place was utterly silent. Yes, surely they would let him go home now.

He turned a corner—and ran smack into Mr Majeika! He screamed and his head fell off.

Mr Majeika yelled out—and yelled again when he saw the head bouncing along the floor.

Phil's body ran one way and his head bounced the other way.

Mr Majeika turned and ran but he couldn't find the way back to his room. He kept taking wrong turnings in the dark and it was a full ten minutes before he had groped his way back to his own room.

Meanwhile Phil had managed to find his head. Without stopping to put it on, he rushed for safety—into the nearest open door he could find.

And this open door just happened (though he didn't know it) to be the door to Mr Majeika's bedroom.

'Phew! my room at last,' murmured Mr Majeika, sinking wearily on to the bed and pulling back the bedclothes so that he could collapse into bed.

From the bed, Phil Spectre's head stared up, terrified, at Mr Majeika.

Thomas and Melanie heard the shrieks and hurried into Mr Majeika's room in their night things, blinking the sleep out of their eyes. 'There *is* a ghost!' gasped Mr Majeika, pointing a shaking hand at Phil.

'Yes,' said Thomas. 'So we can see. And surely ghosts are Walpurgians aren't they?' Mr Majeika nodded. 'So,' went on Thomas, 'why don't you two say hello to each other in the proper way?'

Phil Spectre stared at Thomas, then at Mr Majeika and then he began to smile. 'Apprentice Wizard Majeika?' he said nervously.

Mr Majeika, who had begun to smile too, nodded. 'Apprentice Spook—?'

'Spectre, sir,' said Phil Spectre; and he and Mr Majeika pulled each other's noses, which is how all proper Walpurgians always greet each other.

'But what in the name of Walpurgis are you doing down here, and on Walpurgis Night too?' asked Mr Majeika.

'It was all the Worshipful Wizard's idea,' explained Phil Spectre. '"Off you go," he said, "and cheer up Majeika."'

'Did he?' asked Mr Majeika excitedly. 'Did he really?'

'Just so you wouldn't be alone on Walpurgis Night.'

'Well, well,' said Mr Majeika. And then a thought crossed his mind. 'Apprentice Spook Spectre, you wouldn't like a job, would you?'

'A job, Apprentice Wizard Majeika?' asked Phil Spectre nervously.

'A haunting,' explained Mr Majeika. 'A real permanent haunting. A lovely historical castle, all to yourself. And lots of real people to frighten?'

'A castle? People?' said Phil Spectre anxiously. 'Oh, no—no, not yet. I'm too young.'

'How old are you?' asked Thomas.

'Four hundred and thirty,' said Phil Spectre.

'Well, then,' said Mr Majeika, 'I should have thought you were just about old enough for a real haunting job. Right here, in Chutney Castle.'

Lord Reg and Lady Lillie were rather surprised to be woken in the middle of the night, especially when Mr Majeika explained that he wanted to introduce them to a ghost. But when Lady Lillie had got over her fright, she began to take to Phil.

'Oh, isn't he a little love, Reg?' she cooed.

'He certainly is, my little Pickalillie,' said Lord Reg. 'Just think of all the lovely visitors he'll bring us. The Ghost of Chutney Castle! We can advertise him on all the posters.'

'But I'm a shy ghost,' said Phil nervously to Mr Majeika. 'Tell 'em I'm shy.'

'*I* was shy when I started work as a teacher, Phil,' said Mr Majeika. 'But this Britland life does wonders for you. You'll love it.'

Phil thought for a moment. 'Can I sleep in a turret?' he asked hopefully.

'Of course,' said Lord Reg.

'A really smelly old turret, where no *people* would dare to go?'

'The West Tower is full of mouldy onions that didn't take to pickling,' said Lady Lillie. 'No one ever sets foot there.'

'Oh, Mr Majeika,' said Phil Spectre, smiling. 'Just think of it, a real turret of my own. Why, I can gibber in the moonlight and go flying out among the bats. I just can't wait!'

*

'Seems Phil Spectre isn't coming back,' said the Worshipful Wizard. 'Majeika has applied for a permanent absence for him. He's got a real haunting job.'

'Splendid,' said Wizard Thymes. 'We ought to mark that on Majeika's Progress chart. He's doing really well this term.'

'And apparently he and Phil Spectre had a jolly Walpurgis Night together, eating—what was it he said?—pickled onions.'

'Ugh!' said Wizard Thymes. 'No accounting for Britland taste. Give me a bogweed sandwich any day.'

*   *   *

HUMPHREY CARPENTER brings a lot of knowledge of the world of magic to his stories, having written biographies of two of the most famous writers of fantasy fiction, J. R. R. Tolkien and C. S. Lewis. Reading their books prepared him for creating the adventures of the little wizard, Mr Majeika, who has now become famous in print and on television. Carpenter, who was born in Oxford, was educated—appropriately— at the Dragon School and for a time played in a band called Vile Bodies. He then worked for the BBC before becoming a full-time writer. Carpenter introduced his most popular character in *Mr Majeika* in 1984 and this has been followed by almost a dozen more titles including *Mr Majeika and the Haunted Hotel* (1987) and *Mr Majeika and the Ghost Train* (1994). He has also found time to run a drama group for young people called The Mushy Pea Theatre Company, and enjoy his hobby of exploring decaying railway junctions. A man with a wonderful sense of humour, Humphrey Carpenter knows how children think and believes *he* is more than a little like Mr Majeika. 'He is me and is halfway between the child and the adult world. He sides by instinct with children and is not exactly anti-authoritarian, but is quite happy if authority is upset.'

GRIMNIR AND THE SHAPE-SHIFTER

Alan Garner

There have been a number of evil wizards written about in history books and several awesome characters in fiction: for example, the cruel Gorice in The Worm Ouroborus *by E. R. Eddison (1922), the monster of evil, Grimnir, in Alan Garner's* The Weirdstone of Brisingamen *(1960) and, of course, Voldemort, the Lucifer among wizards, who killed Harry Potter's parents before the opening of the first novel,* Harry Potter and the Philosopher's Stone *(1997), and also inflicted the lightning-shaped scar on the boy's forehead. He will surely make more attempts on the young wizard's life in later stories. Grimnir, 'The Hooded One', was also once a wise man who was tempted into practising the forbidden arts of black magic and is now consumed with evil ambitions. As is so often the case with wizards gone wrong, Grimnir has formed an alliance with an equally scheming wizardess, Selina Place, the chief witch of the Morthbrood, and feared because of her reputation as 'Old Shape-shifter'. In this story, the pair have seized the Firefrost Stone and plan to seal it in a magic circle so that they can use its power. Unknown to them, however, two smart kids, Colin and Susan—from whom the tear-shaped stone was stolen—and who know a lot about black and white magic, thanks to their schooling by the great wizard,*

Cadellin Silverbrow, have tracked them to Selina's gaunt, gabbled mansion, St Mary's Clyffe, where terrible forces are about to be unleashed . . .

* * *

The room was long, with a high ceiling, painted black. Round the walls and about the windows were draped black velvet tapestries. The bare wooden floor was stained a deep red. There was a table on which lay a rod, forked at the end, and a silver plate containing a mound of red powder. On one side of the table was a reading-stand, which supported an old vellum book of great size, and on the other stood a brazier of glowing coals. There was no other furniture of any kind.

Grimnir looked on with much bad grace as Shapeshifter moved through the ritual of preparation. He did not like witch-magic: it relied too much on clumsy nature spirits and the slow brewing of hate. He preferred the lightning stroke of fear and the dark powers of the mind.

But certainly this crude magic had weight. It piled force on force, like a mounting wave, and overwhelmed its prey with the slow violence of an avalanche. If only it were a quick magic! There could be very little time left now before Nastrond acted on his rising suspicions, and then . . . Grimnir's heart quailed at the thought. Oh, let him but bend this stone's power to his will, and Nastrond should see a true Spirit of Darkness arise; one to whom Ragnarok, and all it contained, would be no more than a ditch of noisome creatures to be bestridden and ignored.

But how to master the stone? It had parried all his
rapier thrusts, and, at one moment, had come near
to destroying him. The sole chance now lay in this
morthwoman's witchcraft, and she must be watched;
it would not do for the stone to become *her* slave.
She trusted him no more than could be expected,
but the problem of how to rid himself of her when
she had played out her part in his schemes was not
of immediate importance. The shadow of Nastrond
was growing large in his mind, and in swift success
alone could he hope to endure.

With black sand, which she poured from a leather
bottle, Shape-shifter traced an intricately patterned
circle on the floor. Often she would halt, make a sign
in the air with her hand, mutter to herself, curtsy,
and resume her pouring. She was dressed in a black
robe, tied round with scarlet cord, and on her feet
were pointed shoes.

So intent on her work was the Morrigan, and so
wrapped in his thoughts was Grimnir, that neither of
them saw the two pairs of eyes that inched round the
side of the window.

The circle was complete. Shape-shifter went to the
table and picked up the rod.

'It is not the hour proper for summoning the aid
we need,' she said, 'but if what you have heard contains even a grain of the truth, then we see that we
must act at once, though we could have wished for
a more discreet approach on your part.' She indi-
cated the grey cloud that pressed against the glass,
now empty of watching eyes. 'You may well attract
unwanted attention.'

At that moment, as if in answer to her fears, a

distant clamour arose on the far side of the house. It was the eerie baying of hounds.

'Ah, you see! They are restless: there *is* something on the wind. Perhaps it would be wise to let them seek it out; they will soon let us know if it is aught beyond their powers—as well it may be! For if we do not have Ragnarok and Fundindelve upon our heads before the day is out, it will be no thanks to you.'

She stumped round the corner of the house to the outbuilding from which the noise came. Selina Place was uneasy, and out of temper. For all his art, what a fool Grimnir could be! And what risks he took! Who, in their senses, would come so obviously on such an errand? Like his magic, he was no match for the weirdstone of Brisingamen. She smiled; yes, it would take the old sorcery to tame *that* one, *and* he knew it, for all his fussing in Llyn-dhu. 'All right, all right! We're coming! Don't tear the door down!'

Behind her, two shadows moved out of the mist, slid along the wall, and through the open door.

'Which way now?' whispered Susan.

They were standing in a cramped hall, and there was a choice of three doors leading from it. One of these was ajar, and seemed to be a cloakroom.

'In here, then we'll see which door she goes through.'

Nor did they delay, for the masculine tread of Selina Place came to them out of the mist.

'Now let us do what we can in haste,' she said as she rejoined Grimnir. 'There may be nothing threatening, but we shall not feel safe until we are master of the stone. Give it to us now.'

Grimnir unfastened a pouch at his waist, and from

it drew Susan's bracelet. Firefrost hung there, its bright depths hidden beneath a milky veil.

The Morrigan took the bracelet and placed it in the middle of the circle on the floor. She pulled the curtains over the windows and doors, and went to stand by the brazier, whose faint glow could hardly push back the darkness. She took a handful of powder from the silver plate and, sprinkling it over the coals, cried in a loud voice:

'*Demoriel, Carnefiel, Caspiel, Amenadiel!!*'

A flame hissed upwards, filling the room with ruby light. Shape-shifter opened the book and began to read.

'*Vos onmes it ministri odey et destructiones et seratores discorde . . .*'

'What's she up to?' said Susan.

'I don't know, but it's giving me gooseflesh.'

'*. . . eo quod est noce vose coniurase ideo vos conniro et deprecur . . .*'

'Colin, I . . .'

'Sh! Keep still!'

'*. . . et odid fiat mier alve . . .*'

Shadows began to gather about the folds of velvet tapestries in the farthest corners of the room.

For thirty minutes Colin and Susan were forced to stand in their awkward hiding-place, and it took less than half that time for the last trace of enthusiasm to evaporate. They were where they were as the result of an impulse, an inner urge that had driven them on without thought of danger. But now there was time to think, and inaction is never an aid to courage. They would probably have crept away and tried to find Cadellin, had not a dreadful sound of snuffling, which passed frequently beneath the cloakroom window, made them most unwilling to open the outer door.

And all the while Shape-shifter's chant droned on, rising at intervals to harsh cries of command.

'Come, Haborym! Come, Haborym! Come, Haborym!'

Then it was that the children began to feel the dry heat that was soon to become all but intolerable. It bore down upon them until the blood thumped in their ears, and the room spun sickeningly about their heads.

'Come, Orobas! Come, Orabas! Come, Orabas!'

Was it possible? For the space of three seconds the children heard the clatter of hoofs upon bare boards, and a wild neighing rang high in the roof.

'Come, Nambroth! Come, Nambroth! Come, Nambroth!'

A wind gripped the house by the eaves, and tried to pluck it from its sandstone roots. Something rushed by on booming winds. The lost voices of the air called to each other in the empty rooms, and the mist clung fast and did not stir.

'*Coniuro et confirmo super vos potentes in nomi fortis, metuendissimi, infandi . . .*'

Just at the moment when Susan thought she must faint, the stifling heat diminished enough to allow them to breathe in comfort; the wind died, and a heavy silence settled on the house.

After minutes of brooding quiet a door opened, and the voice of Selina Place came to the children from outside the cloakroom. She was very much out of breath.

'And . . . *we* say the stone . . . will . . . be safe. Nothing . . . can reach it . . . from . . . outside. Come away . . . this is a dangerous . . . brew. Should it boil over . . . and we . . . near, that . . . would be the end . . . of us. Hurry. The force is growing . . . it is not safe to watch.'

Mistrustfully, and with many a backward glance, Grimnir joined her, and they went together through the doorway on the opposite side of the hall, and their footsteps died away.

'Well, how do we get out of *this* mess?' said Colin. 'It looks as though we're stuck here until she calls these animals off, and if she's going to do any more of the stuff we've been listening to, I don't think I want to wait that long.'

'Colin, we can't go yet! My Tear's in that room, and we'll never have another chance!'

The air was much cooler now, and no sounds, strange or otherwise, could be heard. And Susan felt that insistent tugging at her inmost heart that had brushed aside all promises and prudence when she stared at the mist from the bridge by the station.

'But Sue, didn't you hear old Place say that it wasn't safe to be in there? And if *she's* afraid to stay it must be dangerous.'

'I don't care; I've got to try. Are you coming? Because if not, I'm going by myself.'

'Oh . . . all right! But we'll wish we'd stayed in here.'

They stepped out of the cloakroom and cautiously opened the left-hand door.

The dull light prevented them from seeing much at first, but they could make out the table and the reading desk, and the black pillar in the centre of the floor.

'All clear!' whispered Susan.

They tiptoed into the room, closed the door, and stood quite still while their eyes grew accustomed to the light: and then they saw.

The pillar was alive. It climbed from out the circle that Selina Place had so laboriously made, a column of oily smoke; and in the smoke strange shapes moved. Their forms were indistinct, but the children could see enough to wish themselves elsewhere.

Even as they watched the climax came. Faster and faster the pillar whirled, and thicker and thicker the dense fumes grew, and the floor began to tremble, and the children's heads were of a sudden full of mournful voices that reached them out of a great and terrible distance. Flecks of shadow, buzzing like flies, danced out of the tapestries and were sucked into the reeking spiral. And then, without warning, the base of the column turned blue. The buzzing rose to a demented whine—and stopped. The whole swirling mass shuddered as though a brake had been savagely applied, lost momentum, died, and drooped like the ruin of a mighty tree. Silver lightnings ran upwards through the smoke: the column wavered, broke, and collapsed into the ball of fire that rose to engulf it. A voice whimpered close by the children and passed through the doorway behind them. The blue light waned, and in its place lay Firefrost, surrounded by the scattered remnants of Shape-shifter's magic circle.

Colin and Susan stood transfixed. Then slowly, as if afraid that the stone would vanish if she breathed or took her eyes off it, Susan moved forward and picked it up.

In the silence she unclasped the bracelet and fastened it about her wrist. She could not believe what she was doing. This moment had haunted her dreams for so many months, and there had been so many bitter awakenings.

In a small room crammed under the eaves Selina Place and Grimnir waited. Both were keyed to an almost unendurable pitch. They knew well the price of failure. Not once in a thousand years had any of their kind disobeyed the charge of Nastrond, but all at some time had stood in the outer halls of Ragnarok and looked on the Abyss. Thus did Nastrond bind evil to his will.

'It cannot be long now,' said the Morrigan. 'Within five minutes the stone must . . .'

A trail of smoke drifted under the door and floated across the room, and a bubbling sound of tears accompanied it. The Morrigan jumped from her chair: her eyes were wild, and there was sweat on her brow.

'*Non licet abire!*' She threw her arms wide to bar the way. '*Coniuro et confirmo super . . .*' But the smoke curled round her towards the hearth, and leapt into the chimney mouth. A wind sighed mournfully past the windows, and was still.

'No! No,' she mumbled, groping for the door; but Grimnir had already flung it open and was rushing along the corridors to the stairs. He was halfway down the first flight when there was the sound of breaking glass, and the staircase was momentarily in shadow as a dark figure blocked the window at its head. The Morrigan's harsh voice cried out in fear, and Grimnir turned with the speed and menace of a hungry spider.

The noise roused Colin and Susan from their trance. Again the Morrigan shrieked.

'Here, let's get out of this!' said Colin, and he pulled his sister into the hall. 'As soon as we're outside run like mad: I'll be right behind you!'

Quite a hullabaloo was breaking out upstairs, and most of the sounds were by no means pleasant; at least they made the other hazard seem less formidable—until Colin opened the door. There was a rasping growl, and out of the mist came a shape that sent the children stumbling backwards into the house, and before they could close the door the hound of the Morrigan crossed the threshold and was revealed in all its malignity.

It was like a bull terrier; except that it stood four feet high at the shoulder, and its ears, unlike the rest of the white body, were covered with coarse red hair. But what set it apart from all others was the fact that, from pointed ears to curling lip, its head and muzzle were blank. There were no eyes.

The beast paused, swinging its wedge-shaped head from side to side, and snuffling wetly with flared nostrils, and when it caught the children's scent it moved towards them as surely as if it had eyes. Colin and Susan dived for the nearest door, and into what was obviously a kitchen, which had nothing to offer them but another door.

'We'll have to risk it,' said Susan: 'that thing'll be

through in a second.' She put no trust in the flimsy latch, which was rattling furiously beneath the scrabbling of claws. But as she spoke they heard another sound; footsteps rapidly drawing near to the other door! And then the latch did give way, and the hound was in the room.

Colin seized a kitchen chair. 'Get behind me,' he whispered.

At the sound of his voice the brute froze, but only for an instant: it had found its bearings.

'Can we reach a window?' Colin dared not take his eyes off the hound as it advanced upon them.

'No.'

'Is there another way out?'

'No.'

He was parrying the lunges and snappings with the chair, but it was heavy, and his arms ached.

'There's a broom cupboard, or something, behind us, and the door's ajar.'

'What good will that do?'

'I don't know: but Grimnir may not notice us, or the dog may attack him, or . . . oh, anything's better than this!'

'Is it big enough?'

'It goes up to the ceiling.'

'Right. Get in.'

Susan stepped inside and held the door open for Colin as he backed towards it. The hound was biting at the chair legs and trying to paw them down. Wood crunched and splinters flew, and the chair drooped in Colin's hands, but he was there. He hurled the chair at the snarling head, and fell backwards into the cupboard. Susan had a vision of a red tongue lolling out of a gaping mouth, and of fangs flashing white, inches from her face, before she slammed the door; and at the same moment, she heard the kitchen door being flung open. Then she fainted.

Or, at least, she *thought* she had fainted. Her stomach turned over, her head reeled, and she seemed to be falling into the bottomless dark. But *had* she fainted? Colin bumped against her in struggling to right himself: she could feel that. And the back of the cupboard was pressing into her. She pinched herself. No, she had not fainted.

Colin and Susan stood rigidly side by side, nerving themselves for the moment when the door would be opened. But the room seemed unnaturally still: not a sound could they hear.

'What's up?' whispered Colin. 'It's too quiet out there.'

'Shh!'

'I can't see a keyhole anywhere, can you? There should be one somewhere.' He bent forward to feel.

'*Ouch*!!'

Colin let out a yell of surprise and pain, and this time Susan nearly *did* faint.

'Sue! There's no door!'

'Wh-what?'

'No door! It's something that feels like smooth rock going past very quickly, and I've skinned my hand on it. That's why my ears have been popping! We're in a lift!'

Even as he spoke, the floor seemed to press against their feet, and a chill, damp air blew upon their faces, and they were aware of a silence so profound that they could hear their hearts beating.

'Where on earth are we?' said Colin.

'It's probably more like where *in* earth are we!'

Susan knelt on the floor of the cupboard and stretched out her hand to where the door had been. Nothing. She reached down, and touched wet rock.

'Well, there's a floor. Let's have our bike lamps out and see what sort of place this is.'

They took off their knapsacks and rummaged around among the lemonade and sandwiches.

By the light of the lamps they saw that they were at the mouth of a tunnel that stretched away into the darkness.

'Now what do we do?'

'We can't go back, can we, even if we wanted to?'

'No,' said Susan, 'but I don't like the look of this.'

'Neither do I, but we haven't really much choice; come on.'

They shouldered their packs and started off along the tunnel, but seconds later a slight noise brought them whirling round, their hearts in their mouths.

'That's torn it!' said Colin gazing up at the shaft, into which the cupboard was disappearing. 'They'll be on to us in no time now.'

The children went as fast as they could, stumbling over the uneven floor, and bruising themselves against the walls. The air was musty, and within a minute they were gasping as though they had run a mile, but on they sped, with two thoughts in their heads—to escape from whatever was following them, and to find Cadellin . . .

*   *   *

ALAN GARNER is famous for having utilised the legend of the 'Wizard of Alderley' in Cheshire where he and his family have lived for generations as the inspiration for his pair of classic fantasy novels, *The Weirdstone of Brisingamen* (1960) and its sequel, *The Moon of Gomrath* (1963). These books, and his later fantasies, *Elidor* (1965), *The Owl Service* (1967) which was awarded the Carnegie Medal, and *Red Shift* (1973) filmed for television five years later, have established him as one of the masters of the genre. As a result, Alderley Edge has now become a popular spot with visitors of all ages who are keen to trace the legend—and there is even a Wizard Restaurant at Nether Alderley. Alan Garner has always insisted that he doesn't invent his stories, but finds them in landscapes and among the artifacts of ancient history, especially those of his native Cheshire.

DARK OLIVER

Russell Hoban

One of the bad things about school is bullies. Lots of kids have enemies and have to put up with abuse and bad language for no particular reason expect they may have unknowingly crossed someone. Those with the power of magic are no different—though they may just have the means to put a stop to bullying. In this next story, Oliver's problem is a bigger boy called Geoffrey. Oliver is ten and Geoffrey is two years older and likes to amuse himself by twisting the smaller boy's arms and rubbing his head in painful ways. Geoffrey thinks it is all a bit of a laugh and is often taunting Oliver with a little song that goes, 'Olive Oil had a boil right on the bottom of his bum'. But Oliver is not like other boys. He has strange dreams and these get even stranger when he goes on holiday with his mum and dad to the Greek island of Paxos. Something awaits him there that will open his eyes to the wonder of magic and at the same time solve the worst of his problems . . .

*   *   *

Oliver sometimes dreamed a face that was green like pale fire, black like earth and ashes. It was huge, this face, and it was all around him as if it were the inside of an endless tube that slowly turned as he fell endlessly through it. And a sadness, an ache in the throat, a loss. What name was there to call? Who was gone? Oliver was ten.

The playground at school was for Oliver a grey place of rage and boy-sweat and Geoffrey. Geoffrey was two years older and four inches taller and he twisted Oliver's arm and rubbed his head in painful ways. Oliver fought him and lost. Geoffrey called him 'Olive Oil'. Geoffrey sang:

> *'Olive Oil had a boil*
> *right on the bottom of his bum.'*

At the end of the summer term Oliver and his mother and father flew to Corfu and there they boarded a boat for the island of Paxos where they'd rented a house. The name in Greek letters on the bows of the boat was PERSEPHONEIA.

The air was clear, the sun was hot, the engine droned, the sunlight danced in dazzling points on the blue sea. There were stone fortresses, the coast was mountainous, on the upper deck a man played a bouzouki. The boat was full of people eating, drinking, smoking, playing cards. Sun-glints moved slowly across the glasses and the bottles of beer and cloudy lemonade on the bar. On the lower deck were a lorry and two cars and a motorcycle; there were a goat and a donkey; there was a cockerel with bronzey and green and red feathers, it looked at the mountains and crowed. Oliver's father stood in the bow and looked down at the constant parting of the water that slid along the sides and joined the white wake marbling astern. His mother, her bare legs and sandalled feet already brown from afternoons at the

Hurlingham Club, sat on a hatch cover, reading and smoking.

Oliver was listening past the drone of the engine, the slap of the bow wave, the jangling of the bouzouki: he was listening to the silvery flicker of olive trees in the sunlight, the olive trees of the island. It took so long to get there, hours and hours over the sea to the island.

When the boat dropped anchor in the harbour at Gaios and the chain rattled through the hawsepipe Oliver looked up at the hills and terraces beyond the red-tiled roofs of the town. 'What kind of trees are those?' he said. 'The silvery ones.'

'Those are olive trees,' said his mother.

'Persephoneia,' whispered Oliver.

'What are you whispering?'

'Nothing.'

The house looked as if it had been stained long ago with the juice of pomegranates. It had a red pantiled roof, it had a flagged courtyard. There was a table under a grape arbour; there were orange trees and a pomegranate tree. Oliver was astonished at the pomegranates, that this fruit he had read about in fairy tales should actually be growing on a tree where he was. He'd eaten pomegranate seeds at home but now as he held the fruit in his hand it was an orangey-red world of unknownness.

Oliver's father cut a pomegranate into thirds and offered one to Oliver's mother. She looked at him as she bit into it but said nothing. For a moment the other two thirds lay on the white plate among drops of red juice. From a distance came the gigantic braying of a donkey, to Oliver it was the sound of something shut out and banished from happiness: it was a black sound that lay on the white plate with the two thirds of pomegranate and the drops of red juice.

'Persephone', said Oliver, 'ate seven pomegranate seeds in the realm of the dead and because of that she has to spend three months of every year down there with Hades and the earth is barren until she returns.'

'How many seeds have you eaten?' said his father to his mother.

'Too many,' she said.

Years later Oliver remembered some details and forgot others. He remembered tins of NOYNOY evaporated milk, they had a label with a picture of a pretty young Dutch woman breast-feeding a child, in the background a canal and windmills; he remembered bottles of gin with unknown labels, unremembered names; pistachio nuts; black wrinkled olives and goat cheese; mosquito-averting spirals of some green compressed substance that burned with the dark holiday smell of lost childhood.

He remembered a tiny dead scorpion on the floor of a cupboard. He remembered a polychaete seaworm; magnified by the clear water, it was mythical-looking, pink and purple, its body fringed with undulating black bristles that moved it over the pale stones; the idea of it was huge.

There were three Swedish girls who wore no tops, their breasts were large and buoyant; they swam together like a sign of the zodiac.

One day a young woman in a black wet-suit speared an octopus. She slid it off the spear, took it by a couple of its arms and beat it to death on a flat rock, spattering Oliver with briny drops. Each time the octopus struck the rock it gripped it with its free arms, they came away with a sound like kisses.

Oliver and his mother went to the beach every day, his father less often. Oliver's mother swam, sun-bathed, smoked, wrote letters, read mysteries while his father sat at the table under the grape arbour, reading Marlowe's *Doctor Faustus* and making notes for his next book. In the evenings the two of them drank gin by candlelight.

Every day the sunshine was as flat as a postcard. Old women in black sat knitting outside the shops. At the harbour wall the old boatmen looked up from their boats as the near-naked summer women passed by.

Water for the house came from a cistern that was a little square edifice the same colour as the house, with steps going up to the low flat top of it. Rainwater supplied the cistern through a long pipe from the roof gutters of the house. Whenever a tap was turned on or the toilet flushed, the pump in the cistern gasped and panted as it laboured to bring water to where it was wanted.

Lying in his bed at night Oliver heard the crowing of a cock while the pump howled in the dark. He remembered the condemned voice of the donkey, the red juice of the pomegranate, the green and black face of his dream. At night this month of August was like a great animal of unknown shape and colour that turned and turned and turned away.

There were dry stone walls all over the island; they held the earthen terraces to the hillsides; sometimes they encircled single olive trees. Everywhere were stones and fragments of stone with flat surfaces that were good to draw on with a fibre-tip pen. Some were sand-coloured, some grey, some white. Some looked like curtains of stone, some like broken monuments. On the beach and in the water crouched great humped and hollowed ancient sea-worn shapes of stone. They had heard radios playing rock-and-roll and they had heard Orpheus. Lying half-submerged, Oliver held on to them while his body rose and fell with the rocking of the tide. Sometimes he spent hours on the beach bent over his shadow as he gathered hand-sized stones of various rounded shapes. Some of them fitted together in curious ways.

At first Oliver drew monsters and dragons on some of the stones; later he began to write on them. On some of the long-shaped rounded ones he wrote a single word in spirals round and round the stone: Down down down down down down ... or Green green green green ... He also wrote, in the Greek letters he had seen on the boat, the name Persephoneia.

The road that led from the hills down into the town passed between terraces of olive groves. There was rubbish scattered everywhere, people simply threw it down the hillsides. Blue plastic mineral-water bottles were scattered through the olive groves where thrown-away cookers lay rusting. Many of the trees had been planted long, long ago when there were no such things as plastic mineral-water bottles. They twisted their roots into the stony ground of their stone-walled terraces while in their silvery leaves the changing winds, the light of centuries whispered.

There was one particular olive tree that Oliver looked at whenever he passed it. Often there was a black donkey tied to it; sometimes there was a black-and-white goat nearby. The donkey was the one that Oliver had heard while eating the pomegranate under the grape arbour. When it opened wide its jaws and brayed it made a tremendous heehaw that was much too big a sound for an animal of that size; clearly the donkey was a medium for something else. This is my annunciation, said the voice that spoke through the donkey; this is my revelation of something so horrendous that there is no word for it and the voice with which I speak is taken no notice of.

The tree wasn't far from the house; Oliver went to it alone one afternoon. The donkey had wound its rope round and round the tree and now stood silent. The goat looked calmly at Oliver with its strange eyes that were like ochre-grey stones in which were set oblongs of black stone. A cock crowed among the blue plastic mineral-water bottles.

The tree was alive, there were silver leaves whispering in the sunlight, there were black olives growing on it. Yet the trunk was empty, it was only the shell of a tree with darkness inside the ancient twisted shape of it. The thick greenish-grey bark all ridged and wrinkled stood open as if two hands had parted it. The tree wasn't shaped like a woman and yet it was a woman-shaped tree, as if a woman had been wearing the tree and had stepped out of it.

Where is she now? thought Oliver. He looked at the ears of the donkey. What were they listening for? He looked at the eyes of the goat. What did they see that was different from what he saw? The cock crowed again.

'Here?' said Oliver.

The leaves whispered.

'Gone?' said Oliver.

The empty tree held open its darkness to him. The donkey sounded its tremendous heehaw, the goat looked at Oliver, the cock crowed a third time. Oliver stepped closer to the tree. He thought he heard music but he couldn't have said how it sounded. Perhaps it was only the idea of music in his mind.

Oliver was inside the tree, he didn't know how he'd got there. For a moment he saw the stone walls and the olive trees across the road, blue sky and silver leaves, green shade and golden sunlight and a yellow plastic meat grinder lying by the roadside; then everything blurred upward past him, he was falling, falling with a sick feeling in his stomach. There was a great sighing in him and around him; he remembered the eyes of the goat, the ears of the donkey.

Falling, falling, with the darkness leaping inside him like a black frog, Oliver began to cry but it wasn't from fright, he was crying from sadness. With a terrible ache in his throat he was crying for something lost to him, he didn't know what. And all the time he was falling and wondering when he'd be smashed like an egg dropped from the nest.

A name was roaring in him, bellowing in him: PER-
SEPHONEIA. He thought his skull would burst from
it, he thought his bones would break from it. He was
still falling, he was nowhere, there was nothing but
blackness, and into the blackness there came the idea
of the face that he sometimes saw in his dreams. Was
he thinking it or was it thinking him? Inexplicably it
was all around him as he fell. Bigger and bigger it
grew, blotches of black on pale green, like a rubbing
done on green paper. But the green was more like
pale cold fire. Cold, yes, it was bitter cold, icy cold
and a freezing wind blowing.

Oliver began to know that this was the face of
Hades all around him; there was no end to it, the
stony black and cold green fire of it turning, turning,
a turning hollowness going straight down. Oliver fell
and fell and kept on falling through it while the lips
of Hades slowly moved, his mouth roared silently,
PERSEPHONEIA.

Like the sea flooding a cave the idea of Hades and
Persephone filled Oliver. It was in him that the green
and golden summer of the world was winter for
Hades, his black time, dead time, lost and broken
time without Persephone. Persephone was everything
beautiful and she was gone into the upper world of
sunlight whispering in the olive groves. How could
Hades know that she would ever come back to him?
Why should she want to return to the sombre world
of the dead as his dark queen? The king of the dead
raged and wept in his terror, always turning, turning,
slowly turning the face of his rage below the world.

Still Oliver was falling, and still that slowly turning
face rushed upward from below all around him as

he fell. The idea of it was too hard and heavy for him to hold in his mind, the pain of it was too much for him to bear. 'I think I'm going to die of it,' he said. But he didn't die.

The falling had stopped, the slowly turning face of Hades was gone. Oliver saw the eyes of the goat, he saw the donkey's ears turned back and listening. He heard the crowing of the cock, the whisper of the olive leaves. He was in the greenlit shade of the olive grove. The woman-shaped tree stood before him holding open its emptiness to him. Perhaps nothing had happened?

There was a stone in Oliver's hand that filled it comfortably and had a pleasing heaviness. It was a tawny broken stone with sharp edges and irregular facets that tapered to a triangular base; it looked like abstract sculpture of monumental size, it looked commemorative. There was a shallow concavity where his thumb fitted, and when he removed his thumb and held the stone at a certain angle to the light this hollow filled with the shadow of a great bird of the realm of the dead that stood with its back to him. He knew that it was a bird of power: it was a bird of loss, a winged sorrow for what was gone for ever. The thought of it was suddenly overwhelming and he cried.

Oliver thought of the stone as his Hades stone. He kept it in his pocket during the day and he kept it under his pillow at night. He didn't write on it or draw on it; with his thumb he felt the shape of the shadow-bird. He imagined it spreading its dark wings and he wondered about the unseen face of it.

*

When Oliver and his mother and father came back from Paxos the London streets looked mean and grey.

'Hades,' whispered Oliver.

'"Hell hath no limits,"' said his father, '"nor is circumscribed in one self place; for where we are is hell, and where hell is there must we ever be."'

'Speak for yourself,' said Oliver's mother.

When Oliver went back to school he had the Hades stone in his pocket, fitting his fingers, fitting his thumb.

It was a cold September, the air was grey, the streets were grey, the tarmac of the playground was hard under Oliver's feet.

There was Geoffrey again. 'Hello, Olive Oil,' he said.

Oliver didn't say anything. He saw the olive tree holding open its dark emptiness; with his thumb he felt the shape of the shadow-bird whose face he had not yet seen.

'What's the matter?' said Geoffrey. 'Cat got your tongue?'

Oliver took the stone out of his pocket. 'Do you know where this is from?'

'No. Where's it from?'

'Perhaps you'll find out soon. Hell hasn't got any limits—did you know that? It's wherever we are.'

'I think you've gone right round the twist, Olive Oil.'

'Perhaps you'll go somewhere too.' Oliver wanted to exact something from Geoffrey, wanted Geoffrey to feel the sorrow that he felt without knowing why. 'There's a darkness inside the tree,' he said.

'Sounds like there's a darkness inside your head.'

'Nothing is for ever—summer comes, summer goes. Geoffrey comes . . .'

'But he's jolly well not going, Olive Oil.'

Oliver moved back three steps. He tilted his head, listening to the great voice that spoke through the donkey. 'The darkness is waiting; the donkey says go.'

'You're the donkey and I think what you need is a good thumping.'

Oliver moved three steps to the left. He made his eyes like ochre-grey stones with oblong black stones set in them. 'The goat says go.'

'Baaa,' said Geoffrey. 'Why don't you try to make me go?'

Oliver moved forward three steps. At the back of his throat he crowed silently. 'The cock says go. Because it's time.'

'It's past time, Olive Oil,' said Geoffrey. He drew back his fist.

Oliver held the Hades stone so that the great shadowy bird appeared. He saw the bird rise high into the air, he saw its face that was black like earth and ashes, green like pale fire. 'Time for you to go,' he said to Geoffrey as the shadow bird stooped.

Oliver was all alone, falling endlessly while the slowly turning face of Hades rushed upward all around him. Not endlessly—he had stopped falling and it was the unturning face of the school nurse that he saw as he came awake gasping from the little bottle she held under his nose. The Hades stone was no longer in his hand.

'Are you with us again?' said the nurse.

'What happened?'

'It seems that you fainted after your exertions.'

'What exertions?'

'Geoffrey says you were showing him a judo throw.'

'Where's Geoffrey now?'

'They've taken him to hospital for stitches on his head. The playground is not the place for judo practice. Someone might have been seriously hurt.'

'We won't do it again.'

'I should hope not.'

'Here's your stone back,' said Geoffrey later. 'You know, it's a funny thing. When you bashed me with it I saw a great big face all around me, it was green and black and it kept turning.'

'I've seen that face,' said Oliver.

'Where? When?'

'On the island of Paxos last month.'

'How come you saw it?'

'I can't talk about it.'

'I'll swap you an Iron Maiden cassette for that stone.'

'Sorry, but no.'

'It's got my blood on it.'

'I've got another good stone from Paxos, from the beach; I'll give you that one but you have to stop calling me Olive Oil.'

'OK.'

The autumn term went well for Oliver; the other boys seemed to look at him differently from the way they had before. There was a school play about King Arthur and he was given the part of Merlin.

*   *   *

RUSSELL HOBAN is the author of one of the best modern children's books, *The Mouse and His Child* (1967), about the quest of a clockwork mouse and his son for a home where they no longer need to be re-wound. It is, in fact, one of almost fifty stories he has written for younger readers as well as a number of fantasy novels for adults. Hoban is actually an American who settled in Britain after the Second World War and worked in advertising and television before writing and illustrating the books that have made his reputation. His fascination with the powers of magic became obvious in stories like *The Mole Family's Christmas* (1969) in which a mole is granted his wish for a telescope to see the stars, and *The Sea-Thing Child* (1972) about talking creatures: especially a crab with a haunting face. Russell Hoban sees himself as a magician with words—he likes to say to the reader, 'my next trick is impossible' and then carry it off—just as he has shown in 'Dark Oliver', a tale that reminds me of the young seventeenth-century wizard, Master Oliver, I mentioned in 'The World of Wizardry'.

FINDERS KEEPERS

Joan Aiken

Denzil Gilbert is the new boy at Candlemakers, a rambling old school near Norwich. He's thin and spotty and has a squint which means that nobody is quite sure whether he is talking to them or someone else behind. He boasts a lot and makes up stories about so-called famous people in his family. So it's no surprise that most of the kids don't really like Denzil—although that doesn't appear to bother him too much. After a while, though, it turns out that the one thing Denzil is good at is telling ghost stories. After lights out in the dormitory, he can make anyone's hair stand on end with tales of magic and mystery. But when Denzil and the other pupils go on a trip to a little folklore museum at Strand-next-the-sea, something very weird happens with an exhibit known as the 'Finder'. What everyone wants to know is does it have supernatural powers—as Denzil says—or is it just another of his tall stories . . .

*   *   *

Halfway through the spring term we always have a school trip to the museum at Strand-next-the-Sea. Strand is the nearest town to our school, Candlemakers, which is not far from a village called Far Green. Far Green can hardly be called a place— three houses and a pond; in World War II they moved

the school from London to a big red Victorian
draughty hulk of a mansion here, thinking it would
be safe from bombing because the Germans would
never see it. In fact it's so hard to see that visiting
parents often get lost, and end up in Staithe Cross
or Watchett. The house is in the middle of a kind of
miniature forest: elms packed tight around it like
insulation. A lot of the elms got Dutch disease, so
they look like gloomy old skeletons, but then a whole
grove of young sycamores shot up among the elms.

Apart from the trees round the school, it's flat,
windy country. From the spire of Far Green church
you're supposed to be able to see Norwich, in clear
weather, if you look one way; and if you look the
other way, in foggy weather, you're supposed to be
able to see the spire of Losthope Minster, which vanished under the sea in the great gale of 1609.

The spring term is always dismal. Wind rages in
across the North Sea and rain pours down five days
out of six; the games fields are generally under water,
and so it's cross-country jogging, day after gusty,
drenching day. By mid-term, although Strand is a
bleak little town, and the museum is simply three
rooms of rubbishy odds-and-ends collected by some
nineteenth-century Reverend who had nothing else
to do with his spare time, everybody is quite pleased
to go there. At least it's indoors, under cover. We go
there by school bus, and it makes a bit of a change;
though of course by the time you have been at the
school a few years, you know everything in the
museum as well as the contents of your own desk.

This term I'm speaking of there was a new boy
called Denzil Gilbert. He was a thin, pale-eyed, spotty

character with a rough skin like sandpaper and a slight squint in his left eye, so that you never knew whether he was speaking to you, or to somebody over your shoulder. Nobody liked him much, but that didn't seem to bother him; he was wonderfully self-satisfied and would talk away endlessly about himself to anybody who cared to listen. A lot of the stories he told were just plain lies: that his father had won the Nobel Prize for poetry and his grandmother was a famous actress who had played Lady Macbeth with Sir Henry Irving, his grandfather was Lord Chancellor of England and his family had come to England with the Normans. Anybody who could be bothered to check in Who's Who or the encyclopedia would find that most of his tales just weren't so, except for a tiny grain of truth somewhere at the bottom. By the middle of the term nobody took much notice of his boasting.

Denzil was the kind of character who, because he was not interesting in himself, always took care to have rather uncommon possessions, so that he could show them off and get a bit of prestige that way. He had a set of Maundy money—a tiny silver penny, and a twopenny, threepenny, and fourpenny piece; he had a metal powder-horn studded over with bits of turquoise and red coral which he said had belonged to King James I (though in my opinion, if James I had a powder-horn, it would be a fancier-looking article than Denzil's); he had a fossil that he said came from Mars, and a big cowrie in which you were supposed to be able to hear the Indian Ocean roaring; and a little soapstone ink-well that (according to Denzil) had belonged to an old Chinese poet called

Li Po, and anyone who used it would be able to write top-class Chinese poetry. And he had a Malay kris, and a piece of rose-quartz, and a leaf from a Handkerchief Tree, and a lot of nice old green marbles.

People laughed at Denzil's stories about his possessions, of course, but they were interested, and used to ask to look at them, and he was always pleased to display them; and before long—you know how it is at school—specially if a person is rather unpopular—several of the things went missing, in particular the set of tiny silver Maundy Money pieces. Denzil was very upset about that. They had gone out of a tiny silver snuffbox which he kept on his chest-of-drawers in his dormitory.

Of course Jasper, the headmaster, got to hear about it, and he made a statement after prayers, and asked if anybody knew where they were. No one said a word. Jasper was very angry—partly with Denzil, because he said the top of a chest-of-drawers was a stupid place to keep something so valuable, it was putting unfair temptation in people's way. And the end of it was, that a new rule was made: all valuables had to be handed in to Sally Lunn, the Matron. So Denzil had to part with his quartz and ink-well, though he was allowed to keep the cowrie and the Martian fossil, because nobody believed they were what he said.

It was all awkward and uncomfortable, and didn't make Denzil any more popular, as you can imagine.

One thing he was good at, though, was telling ghost stories, when prep was finished and we were all huddled round the dining-room stove; or at night after lights-out. Then he'd have everybody's hair standing on end with tales of the drowned Danish warriors caught by the tide on Saltwagon Marsh after they had been deliberately misdirected by a village boy; the dripping-wet Danes rise up, he said, out of their muddy graves on the last night of May and go looking for that boy to have their revenge, so watch out! And there was another good story about the sunken forest of Losthope, and the awful forest Things that come slithering out, sometimes, in winter gales, when the waves are so huge, up and down, that stumps of the rotted, fossilised trees can still be seen. Or so it's said. And there was a story about giant African bees, moving northwards through Europe, in black crowds a million strong, killing everything on the way.

But none of the stories Denzil Gilbert told us were any stranger than what happened to him.

On this particular Saturday Sally Lunn announced at breakfast that we'd be going to Strand-next-the-Sea museum after lunch, and all the people who'd been there four or five times before gave their usual groan of boredom. But Denzil looked quite bright-eyed and keen. Biddy Frazer was so rash as to ask why. I was surprised, because she was generally one of the first to snub him; she was Scotch, and down-to-earth, and a monitor, and said his stories were silly rubbish.

Denzil said, 'My father was born in Strand-next-the-Sea. Our old family house is there.'

'Then why aren't you a day-boy?'

Biddy's tone was wistful. Hours less of Denzil every-day, she was plainly thinking.

'My grandfather sold the house. And we've always

lived abroad. My father's professor of English at Addis Ababa University.' This was true; one of the things Denzil hadn't invented.

After lunch the rattly old blue bus trundled on to the gravel turnaround in front of the main school house, and we all splashed out through the rain and climbed on board, with the usual moans and grumbles and ribald jokes about where we'd rather have been going.

Nobody wanted to sit with Denzil, so he ended up sitting by Tom Oakenshaw the English master, who could be very sarcastic, but was still being fairly patient with Denzil, as he was a new boy, and prepared to listen to his tall tales without too obvious an expression of disbelief.

The old bus went ploughing along the flat fen roads, throwing up sheets of water, under the huge grey wet windy sky. I was sitting behind Denzil and Oakie, and could hear Denzil shooting a line about his family.

'The Gilberts have lived in Strand-next-the-Sea since the twelfth century.'

'I'm not certain that Strand was there in the twelfth century,' said Oakie mildly. 'The sea was farther out, then, you know.'

'Oh, well, my family have been in these parts since then, anyway,' said Denzil, making a quick comeback. 'Some of them went on crusades from here. There was an ancestor of mine buried in Losthope Minster—Sir Geoffroi de Guilbert; there's a picture of his monument in a book called Lost Curiosities of East Anglian Architecture.'

'Really?' says Oakie. 'I have that book back at

school. I'll look up your ancestor when we get back.'

Biddy, beside me on the seat behind, was stifling her laughter and giving me pokes, because she was ready to bet that none of Denzil's story was true and Oakie would soon find that out. But Denzil seemed quite calm about it.

Presently we rolled into the main square of Strand, which was always a windy, unwelcoming place. One of the four short, wide streets led straight to a row of ever-shifting sand-dunes; another went to the harbour; one had some shops in it; and the fourth had private houses, the church, and the museum.

'Museum first,' said Oakie. 'Then you can spend your pocket-money and have a run on the beach, if it isn't raining too hard.'

We all slouched, two by two, along Staithe Street to the museum which was in a red-brick Georgian building called Acre House. As soon as Denzil arrived in front of it he struck a dramatic attitude and exclaimed, 'The home of my ancestors!'

Most people sniggered, and Oakie hustled us inside.

As I said, there are three rooms. One is full of old agricultural and kitchen utensils, ploughs and churns and butterpats and mangles. The metal things are rusty and the wooden ones are worm-eaten, and unless you are a history enthusiast it's pretty boring.

Another room has a lot of stuffed birds, and local plants growing in tubs, and a big geological scale-model of the country round about; that's the room I like best.

The third room has clothes and costumes, and a

huge old dolls' house, and newspapers left over from the eighteenth century. Most of the girls spend the whole visit in there.

Biddy went off to the costume room, after whispering to me that she was going to faint in ten minutes. Biddy is pale and red-haired, and she is able to make herself faint by putting blotting-paper in her shoes and then concentrating very hard. She doesn't do it too often, or the staff would get wise to it, but this time she said she'd seen Acre House often enough, and she wanted to spend the birthday money her mother had sent. If she fainted, she said, we might be allowed to go and have tea at Polly's Plat, the only café that stays open through the winter.

Denzil went straight into the Costume Room, and I wandered in there, after five minutes or so, because I wanted to watch Biddy stage her faint.

Old Miss Thorpe was doing her stuff. She is the curator; she looks like a lichee nut, pinkish-brown and wrinkled. She must have read about a million books because she can lecture on and on endlessly about every single object in the museum.

'This is a pilgrim's costume,' she was saying. 'You see the cockles or scallop shells on the hat—they show he went to the shrine of St James at Compostella. And the piece of palm shows that he went to the Holy Land too. The hook on the staff was for carrying his bag.

'Now here we have the costume of a crusader. He wore banded mail, a white surcoat to keep off the hot sun, and, as you see, the surcoat has a red cross on it. These are the clothes of Sir Geoffroi de Guilbert, whose family lived at Gippesvicum—that's

Ipswich—and whose descendants built this house in
the eighteenth century.'

'See!' squeaked Denzil proudly to Jane Hall, who
happened to be standing by him. 'Didn't I say this
was the home of my ancestors!'

Miss Thorpe turned round at that, very interested.
'And what may your name be, my boy?'

When he said it was Denzil Gilbert, she was as
pleased as Punch.

'The son of Professor Robert Gilbert? Now, isn't
that perfectly splendid! I've never had a member of
the family in the house before.'

As you can imagine, Denzil just stood there looking
like the rising sun. For once, a story of his had proved
to be true, and you could see it would be a long time
before he would let us forget it.

But Miss Thorpe hadn't finished yet.

'As you're a member of the family,' she went on,
'you may exercise the privilege of *filius donationis*—
this has never happened yet during the time I have
been in charge here, what fun, how topping!' When
Miss Thorpe becomes excited she tends to slip into
Boys' Own Paper language, vintage 1920.

'What is *filius donationis*?' inquired Mr Oakenshaw,
almost as interested as the old girl herself.

'Why, when the house and various bits of property
that went with it were presented as a museum, it was
a condition of the agreement that if ever a descendant of the donor—Sir Giles Gilbert—'

'My grandfather,' sang out Denzil happily.

'If ever a descendant of Sir Giles came in, he might
be allowed to handle the articles in that locked case
over there.'

All heads turned, and all eyes focused on
the locked case, which was not very big, and had
various small dull objects in it—chains and buckles
and seals and coins and links and some dingy little
spoons.

Denzil was not going to pass up a chance like this,
of course.

'Can I handle the things, please?' he said.

'Certainly you can, my boy. Just a moment while I
fetch the key.'

Denzil peered through the glass, looking horribly
self-important; and as many people as cared clustered
round to have a look too.

'There's something written on the spoons—it's in
Latin,' said a girl called Tansy Jones.

'Probably the Latin for "A Present from Norwich",' sniggered Bill Humphrey.

'Dona ex Norvicio,' suggested Jane.

'No it isn't,' said Miss Thorpe, returning with the
key. 'Those are Roman silver spoons, found on the
site of a temple to Faunus, the wood god. Faunus, as
you may know, is also the British god Vaun, and the
Greek god Pan—the letters V, F and P are all inter-
changeable.' Miss Thorpe was well into her stride
now.

'What do the words mean?' Tansy asked.

'Something like "Rejoice in the woods".'

'Have a nice picnic,' muttered Bill.

'All this country was covered by forest at that time,
of course. The temple site is where your school now
stands. Now these are little bits of Roman glass,' said
Miss Thorpe, handing them to Denzil, who tried to
look interested, but found it hard going. 'And these

are ancient British arrow-heads. And this little thing has a curious history—it's called the Finder.'

It was a small metal image of a stocky, smiling little man with a lot of hair and beard, wearing a pointed cap. His feet were backwards-way on.

'Why the Finder?' asked Denzil.

'Because it is supposed to help find lost things. It is an image of the forest god Faunus—or Vaun.'

'Why should he find lost things?'

'Why—I suppose—because things often *are* lost in the woods. In Roman or British days it would prob-ably be children—or dogs or pigs or cattle—and they believed that if you sacrificed to Vaun he would help you find what you had lost. Then later, instead of sacrificing, people began having these little images made and giving them to the temple. This one was dug up in the seventeenth century by a farmer, and it was given the name of the Finder, because, even then, people believed it had the power to find lost things. It was passed from hand to hand all over the district, and in the end it fell into the keeping of your great-great-grandfather Sir Neville Gilbert,' Miss Thorpe told Denzil.

'I jolly well wish it was mine,' he said. 'It's just what I need.'

This was the moment Biddy chose to stage her faint. She did it very artistically, going paper-white, swaying to and fro, then falling on the wood floor with an almighty thump.

'Oh, bless my soul!' said Miss Thorpe, hastily lock-ing the glass case and sticking the key in her cardigan pocket. She and Oakenshaw hoisted Biddy up and dumped heron a wide old leather couch in the front room, and after a minute she opened her eyes, looked round in a dazed way, and said, 'What happened? Where am I?'

'Just lie still, dear, and I'll fetch you a glass of water,' said Miss Thorpe.

'I'd rather a cup of tea,' said Biddy.

'Why don't I take her to Polly's Plat?' I suggested.

But, very annoyingly, Oakie wouldn't let her go to the café. He said she was too groggy to be walking about, and she must sit quietly in the bus while the rest of us spent our pocket money. He escorted Biddy out to the bus and left her in the charge of the driver, Gus Beadle, who never bothered to get out but just stayed on board reading the Sporting Times.

Biddy gave me money to buy her a Mint Sandwich and I went off to the one sweetshop. Denzil tagged along with me. He was still looking as pleased as a dog with two tails, I supposed because of all the attention he'd been getting.

I collected a couple of Coffee Crisps and Biddy's Mint Sandwich, then waited at the counter behind an old character who was buying a packet of pipe tobacco and some extra-strong peppermints. He was feeling about in all his pockets and seemed upset; in fact he had gone almost as white as Biddy.

'What's up, dad?' said the girl at the cash register.

'Lost me five-pun' note,' said the old fellow. 'Oh, drabbit me, what can I have done with the blame thing? I dunno what my old woman'll say—'

'It's under your foot,' said Denzil quietly, as the old man peered hopelessly about the cluttered little shop.

Sure enough, there the note was; he must somehow

have pulled it out of his pocket without noticing, and then stepped on it after it fell. Was he relieved!

He paid for his things, and I bought my stuff, and Denzil got some marshmallows, sickly things—I suspected he bought them because nobody else liked them, so he wouldn't have to give any away; then we walked back to the bus. By now the drizzle had hardened to a steady downpour, given extra zip by a sharp north wind; it was certainly no day for strolling along the sand dunes.

Denzil and I were the last two back on the bus. I handed Biddy her mint sandwich. She was sitting by Oakie, looking sorry for herself, so white that her freckles stood out like rust spots. In fact I began to wonder if perhaps it had been a real faint.

Gus Beadle started his engine, but before he could pull away the bus door flew open. The gale had blown up tremendously fast, as it does in these parts; one minute it's dead calm, five minutes later chimney pots and roof-tiles are sailing down the road.

'Shut the door, will you, Bill,' called Oakie.

Bill, who was next it, thumped it to, but it blew right open again. In the end Gus had to tie it shut with a bit of cord, and Bill had to hold on to it all the way home. The old bus itself nearly lifted off the road, every now and then. It was a real force ten.

Denzil sat by me. He was smirking away to himself still, and once gave me a poke in the ribs and muttered, 'I say! Shall I tell you something?' But I pretended not to hear. I was listening to Oakie, in the seat ahead, who was talking to Biddy and a couple of other girls about the Finder.

'An archaeologist called Murray Parkin borrowed

it from the museum eight or nine years ago, he hoped it might help him find a Saxon treasure-ship like the one at Sutton Hoo.'

'Did it?'

'Not that I ever heard. Unless he went off with the treasure! Perhaps it doesn't work if you borrow it. The seventeenth-century belief was that it had to be given, or stolen.'

'Maybe over the last three hundred years its power got weak from lack of use,' suggested Jane Hall. 'Like a torch battery.'

'Somehow I don't think that would happen.' Oakie took her quite seriously. 'I feel it would be just the other way round. The power would get more and more concentrated. Vaun—Faunus—was a forest god. Quite wild, quite strong. What do you suppose it feels like, if you are a god, not to be worshipped? To have people forget you—ignore you? For hundreds of years?'

'Not very nice, I should think,' said Tansy.

'It would make you angry,' said Jane. 'Specially if, when people *did* remember you, all they wanted was for you to find their lost Aberdeen terrier—'

Biddy shivered, and said in a whining tone, 'I do feel rotten, Mr Oakenshaw! My head aches, and I'm freezing—'

'You're probably coming down with flu,' he said. 'You must go straight to Matron as soon as we get back.'

It began to seem a wonder that we got back at all. The elms and sycamores round the school house were thrashing about as if they were likely to come clean out of the ground, and when Bill undid the bit of cord the bus door flew open so violently that it slammed against the side of the bus and cracked a window. Oakie and I helped Biddy out. She was shivering, and looked green rather than white; the sight of her made me feel a bit queasy too.

The rain was slamming down, so we all bolted into the house. And then we couldn't get the front doors to stay shut. They are two big double ones, heavy oak and iron strapping—the wind kept sucking them open as if they were made of cardboard. Oakie and old Gus had to lock and bolt them before they would hold, and even then they rattled and swayed as if a dinosaur was battering them.

Sally Lunn led Biddy off to the sick bay.

'Can't I go to my room first and get a book?' asked Biddy.

'No, you come with me. One of your friends can bring you a book later,' said the Matron.

The rest of us went in to tea—it is always chocolate swiss roll on Saturday.

Denzil plumped himself down by me.

'Hey! Look what I've got!' he said, showing me something quickly in the palm of his hand.

I had only a hasty glimpse of it but it looked uncommonly like the little black Finder.

'*Christmas*!' I said. 'You don't mean to say you've gone and pinched the—'

'Ssssh! Not so loud. I haven't pinched it.'

'I never heard you ask old Thorpe.'

'I'll return it—maybe,' he said smugly. 'Just as soon as it's found my lost things for me.' He gulped down the last of his tea. 'Come on—want to see it work?'

I didn't, actually; the whole thing gave me a nasty feeling. And the weather didn't help; it was much darker than it should have been, at that time of the afternoon; the wind outside was making a continuous howl like a chain-saw, and doors kept bursting open all over the building.

'Old Jasper's going to be sick as a dog if he finds out what you've done,' I said. 'Stealing from a museum.'

'Oh, don't be such a prig!' said Denzil sharply. 'Besides, I have a right to it. It belonged to my great-great grandfather.'

'And how do we know how *he* came by it?'

Denzil simply walked out of the big dining-room and up the stairs, cupping the little black thing in his hand. 'It's leading me,' he said.

Very unwillingly, I went after him, and so did two or three other people, who had got wind somehow that queer business was afoot.

'Look, *honestly*,' I said, shouting to make myself heard above the howl of the wind, 'I don't think you ought to do this. It's bound to lead to trouble. And— did you hear what Oakie was saying on the bus— if you use this—this kind of thing—you are laying yourself open to forces that—that are better kept separate. It's like touching a live wire. You are putting yourself in its power—'

'Oh, bunk,' said Denzil. 'You don't want me to do it because you're scared of where my things are likely to turn up.' He gave me a nasty grin, looking over his shoulder—as always, I couldn't be sure if his eyes were on me, or on someone else. 'I wonder why *that* is?' he said, and kept on going. 'It wants to go higher up.'

He climbed the next flight of stairs, which led to the girls' dormitories.

'Hey! You're not supposed to go into other people's rooms,' said Tansy, who was tagging along behind. Denzil ignored that. He went into the big room that Biddy Frazer shared with Jane and two others. Nobody was there. One of the windows burst open as Denzil walked in, and all the cubicle curtains streamed sideways like banners. A shower of post-cards and paperback books blew off the tops of dressing-tables.

I struggled to shut and latch the window, and Tansy tried to sort out the cards and put them back where they came from.

Denzil had walked straight to Biddy's corner of the room. A photograph of her family hung on the wall over the bed. He lifted the frame away from the wall, and down fell a thick envelope which had been lodged behind it. Inside were Denzil's little silver Maundy pieces—the penny, twopenny, threepenny, and fourpenny.

'I thought as much!' he said in a satisfied voice.

'You utter beast! You knew they were there!' exclaimed

Tansy. 'Or else you put them there yourself. What a stinking rotten trick. I don't believe Biddy took them.'

'Oh yes she did,' said Denzil, gloating. 'And now I'm going on to find the rest of my things—the powder-horn and the Malay knife and my green marbles.'

He looked round at us all, and his smirk was very unpleasant. 'Who'd have thought that Biddy would be the one to take the coins—being a monitor, and so goody-gumdrop, setting herself up to be better than everybody else. Won't old Jasper be surprised when he hears!'

'You'd better go to him now,' said Jane, very troubled. 'In case—in case suspicion is resting on the wrong person.'

'I'll tell him all right, by and by,' said Denzil. 'Not yet, though.'

'Why not?'

'What, and give the people who took my other things a chance to put them back? Not likely!' And he grinned again, an ugly grin.

Then he looked down again at the little black thing in his hand.

'Vaun, Vaun, little god of the woods,' he chanted, 'help me find my powder-horn and my Malay knife and my green marbles.'

At that moment a voice was heard calling. 'Denzil! Denzil Gilbert! Are you up there?'

'He's up here!' called Jane. 'Who wants him?'

'He's wanted down below.'

Afterwards none of us could agree whose voice we had heard; Jane thought it was Jasper, I thought it was Mr Oakenshaw.

'Oh, blow,' said Denzil. He tucked the Finder into his pocket, with the Maundy money. 'Well, I'll go on with the hunt in a minute; you had all better wait for me here, if you want to watch.'

He stared down the stair. 'I'll just go in here,' he said, and turned into a lavatory which was to the side of the staircase, one step up. He shut the door, and Tansy said,

'Quick! Hadn't we better tell old Jasper what's going on? He won't like it a bit, and he'll be certain to blame us as well—and if we tell him he'll take the Finder away from Denzil before—'

Just at that moment we heard Denzil, who was still inside the loo, give the most extraordinary cry—a kind of howling wail, as if all the breath was being sucked out of his lungs. At the same moment the gale sucked a lot more doors and windows open. The whole building seemed to rock to and fro, and a couple of elms crashed down outside.

'What's up, Denzil?' I called, rattling the doorhandle. 'Are you okay?'

But there was no answer from inside the loo.

In the end we had to get Oakie and Gus Beadle to break down the door. And that was the strangest moment of all, for Denzil wasn't inside. That loo had a tiny round window like a port-hole. A well-fed cat couldn't have got through it. And it was five floors up. But Denzil wasn't there, and we never saw him again.

A memorial service was held for him, nine months later, when he was presumed dead.

During the service I was beside the slab erected to Denzil's great-great-or-whatever-it-was grandfather. So I had plenty of time to read the verse on it, which said:

> *Liste to the winde's lamente*
> *Take heede of its dreare sounde*
> *O Man! Seeke not to finde*
> *Lest ye yourselfe be founde!'*
>
> *This tablet was erected to the memory of*
> *Sir Giles Gilbert,'*
> *who dyed very suddenly in the 65th yeare*
> *of his age, February 27, 1753.*

The Finder, which was discovered on the lavatory floor, was returned to Strand museum and locked up again in the glass case by Miss Thorpe. The Maundy money was not found, but Denzil's clothes and other things were sent off to his parents. The green glass marbles and Malay knife never turned up. And I buried the powder-horn under the elm trees one windy night. It seemed the best thing to do with it.

*   *   *

JOAN AIKEN is the daughter of the famous American novelist, Conrad Aiken, and she began her working life with BBC Radio before starting to write fantasy stories for younger readers. *The Wolves of Willoughby Chase* (1962), an alternative history of England featuring the remarkable heroine Dido Twite, was an immediate success and was later filmed. Twite returned in several later novels including *The Stolen Lake* (1971) in which she encounters King Arthur. Aiken's readership has continued to grow with a stream of short stories, many dealing with magic in a realistic manner, and these can be found collected in volumes such as *More Than You've Bargained For* (1955), *A Small Pinch of Weather* (1969), *A Bundle of Nerves* (1976) and *A Whisper in the Night* (1982). The *Times Educational Supplement* recently said of the author, 'At her best, Joan Aiken has no equal in this genre'—a claim, I think, which 'Finders Keepers' amply justifies.

THE DABBLERS

William Harvey

Lots of schools have a tradition of playing secret games—
special rituals that are passed from one generation of pupils
to the next. A few have 'games' that involve attempts at
magic or trying to summon occult forces and they are pretty
scary, even dangerous. The great ghost story teller, M. R.
James, years ago wrote about one in his creepy tale 'After
Dark In the Playing Fields' and at Hogwarts, the game is
Quidditch, of course, played on broomsticks with Harry Pot-
ter as seeker for his house, Gryffindor. Recently, a book has
appeared, Quidditch Through The Ages *by Kennilwor-*
thy Whisp, in which England wins the Quidditch World
Cup . . . 100 years in the future, though! The game played
in this next story by Burlingham and his friends is, though,
far more sinister. It takes place at Whitchurch Abbey, an
ancient public school in the Eastern Counties of England.
Here there are rumours of midnight processions, unearthly
singing and even animal sacrifices. The secret group are
known as The Dabblers and it is black magic the boys are
interested in, according to Harborough, one of the teachers,
who reveals the facts to two old schoolfriends. The events he
describes seem at first rather like a nightmare from the past.
But the truth is that ancient powers and those who dabble
in them do not necessarily die out . . .

*   *   *

It was a wet July evening. The three friends sat around the peat fire in Harborough's den, pleasantly weary after their long tramp across the moors. Scott, the ironmaster, had been declaiming against modern education. His partner's son had recently entered the business with everything to learn, and the business couldn't afford to teach him. 'I suppose,' he said, 'that from preparatory school to university, Wilkins must have spent the best part of three thousand pounds on filling a suit of plus-fours with brawn. It's too much. My boy is going to Steelborough grammar school. Then when he's sixteen I shall send him to Germany so that he can learn from our competitors. Then he'll put in a year in the office; afterwards, if he shows any ability, he can go up to Oxford. Of course he'll be rusty and out of his stride, but he can mug up his Latin in the evenings as my shop stewards do with their industrial history and economics.'

'Things aren't as bad as you make out,' said Freeman, the architect. 'The trouble I find with schools is in choosing the right one where so many are excellent. I've entered my boy for one of those old country grammar schools that have been completely remodelled. Wells showed in *The Undying Fire* what an enlightened headmaster can do when he is given a free hand and isn't buried alive in mortar and tradition.'

'You'll probably find,' said Scott, 'that it's mostly eyewash; no discipline, and a lot of talk about self-expression and education for service.'

'There you're wrong. I should say the discipline is too severe if anything. I heard only the other day from my young nephew that two boys had been expelled for a raid on a henroost or some such escapade; but I suppose there was more to it than met the eye. What are you smiling about, Harborough?'

'It was something you said about headmasters and tradition. I was thinking about tradition and boys. Rum, secretive little beggars. It seems to me quite possible that there is a wealth of hidden lore passed on from one generation of schoolboys to another that it might be well worth while for a psychologist or an anthropologist to investigate. I remember at my first school writing some lines of doggerel in my books. They were really an imprecation against any one who should steal them. I've seen practically the same words in old monkish manuscripts; they go back to the time when books were of value. But it was on the fly-leaves of Abbott's *Via Latina*, and Lock's *Arithmetic* that I wrote them. Nobody would want to steal those books. Why should boys start to spin tops at a certain season of the year? The date is not fixed by shopkeepers, parents are not consulted, and though saints have been flogged to death I have found no connection between top whipping and the church calendar. The matter is decided for them by an unbroken tradition, handed down, not from father to son, but from boy to boy. Nursery rhymes are not perhaps a case in point, though they are stuffed with odd bits of folklore. I remember being taught a game that was played with knotted handkerchiefs manipulated by the fingers to the accompaniment of a rhyme which began: "Father Confessor, I've come to confess." My instructor, aged eight, was the son of a High Church vicar. I don't know what would have happened if old Tomlinson had heard the last verse:

> *'Father Confessor, what shall I do?'*
> *'Go to Rome and kiss the Pope's toe.'*
> *'Father Confessor, I'd rather kiss you.'*
> *'Well, child, do.'*

'What was the origin of that little piece of doggerel?' asked Freeman. 'It's new to me.'

'I don't know,' Harborough replied. 'I've never seen it in print. But behind the noddings of the knotted handkerchiefs and our childish giggles lurked something sinister. I seem to see the cloaked figure, cat-like and gliding, of one of those emissaries of the Church of Rome that creep into the pages of George Borrow—hatred and fear masked in ribaldry. I could give you other examples, the holly and ivy carols, for instance, which used to be sung by boys and girls to the accompaniment of a dance, and which, according to some people, embody a crude form of nature worship.'

'And the point of all this is what?' asked Freeman.

'That there is a body of tradition, ignored by the ordinary adult, handed down by one generation of children to another. If you want a really good example—a really bad example I should say, I'll tell you the story of the Dabblers.' He waited until Freeman and Scott had filled their pipes and then began.

'When I came down from Oxford and before I was called to the Bar, I put in three miserable years at school teaching.'

Scott laughed.

'I don't envy the poor kids you cross-examined,' he said.

'As a matter of fact, I was more afraid of them than they of me. I got a job as usher at one of Freeman's old grammar schools, only it had not been remodelled and the headmaster was a completely incompetent cleric. It was in the eastern counties. The town was dead-alive. The only thing that seemed to warm the hearts of the people there was a dull smouldering fire of gossip, and they all took turns in fanning the flame. But I mustn't get away from the school. The buildings were old; the chapel had once been the choir of a monastic church. There was a fine tithe barn, and a few old stones and bases of pillars in the headmaster's garden, but nothing more to show where monks had lived for centuries except a dried-up fish pond.

'Late in June at the end of my first year, I was crossing the playground at night on my way to my lodgings in the High Street. It was after twelve. There wasn't a breath of air, and the playing fields were covered with a thick mist from the river. There was something rather weird about the whole scene; it was all so still and silent. The night smelt stuffy; and then suddenly I heard the sound of singing. I don't know where the voices came from nor how many voices there were, and not being musical I can't give you any idea of the tune. It was very ragged with gaps in it, and there was something about it which I can only describe as disturbing. Anyhow I had no desire to investigate. I stood still for two or three minutes listening and then let myself out by the lodge gate into the deserted High Street. My bedroom above the tobacconist's looked out on to a lane that led down to the river. Through the open window I could still hear, very faintly, the singing. Then a dog began to howl, and when after a quarter of an hour it stopped: the June night was again still. Next morning in the masters' common room I asked if any one could account for the singing.

'"It's the Dabblers," said old Moneypenny, the science master, "they usually appear about now."

'Of course I asked who the Dabblers were.

'"The Dabblers," said Moneypenny, "are carol singers born out of their due time. They are certain lads of the village who, for reasons of their own, desire to remain anonymous; probably choir-boys with a grievance, who wish to pose as ghosts. And for goodness' sake let sleeping dogs lie. We've thrashed out the Dabbler controversy so often that I'm heartily sick of it."

'He was a cross-grained customer and I took him at his word. But later on in the week I got hold of one of the junior masters and asked him what it all meant. It seemed an established fact that the singing did occur at this particular time of the year. It was a sore point with Moneypenny, because on one occasion when somebody had suggested that it might be boys from the schoolhouse skylarking he had completely lost his temper.

'"All the same," said Atkinson, "it might just as well be our boys as any others. If you are game next year we'll try to get to the bottom of it."

'I agreed and there the matter stood. As a matter of fact when the anniversary came round I had forgotten all about the thing. I had been taking the lower school in prep. The boys had been unusually rest-less—we were less than a month from the end of term—and it was with a sigh of relief that I turned into Atkinson's study soon after eight to borrow an umbrella, for it was raining hard.

' "By the by," he said, "to-night's the night the Dabblers are due to appear. What about it?"

'I told him that if he imagined that I was going to spend the hours between then and midnight in patrolling the school precincts in the rain, he was greatly mistaken.

' "That's not my idea at all," he said. "We won't set foot out of doors. I'll light the fire; I can manage a mixed grill of sorts on the gas ring and there are a couple of bottles of beer in the cupboard. If we hear the Dabblers we'll quietly go the round of the dormitories and see if any one is missing. If they are, we can await their return."

'The long and short of it was that I fell in with his proposal. I had a lot of essays to correct on the Peas-ants' Revolt—fancy kids of thirteen and fourteen being expected to write essays on anything—and I could go through them just as well by Atkinson's fire as in my own cheerless little sitting-room.

'It's wonderful how welcome a fire can be in a sodden June. We forgot our lost summer as we sat beside it smoking, warming our memories in the glow from the embers.

' "Well," said Atkinson at last, "it's close on twelve. If the Dabblers are going to start, they are due about now." He got up from his chair and drew aside the curtains.

' "Listen!" he said. Across the playground, from

the direction of the playing-fields, came the sound of singing. The music—if it could be called such— lacked melody and rhythm and was broken by pauses; it was veiled, too, by the drip, drip of the rain and the splashing of water from the gutter spouts. For one moment I thought I saw lights moving, but my eyes must have been deceived by reflections on the window pane.

' "We'll see if any of our birds have flown," said Atkinson. He picked up an electric torch and we went the rounds of the dormitories. Everything was as it should be. The beds were all occupied, the boys all seemed to be asleep. It was a quarter-past twelve by the time we got back to Atkinson's room. The music had ceased; I borrowed a mackintosh and ran home through the rain.

'That was the last time I heard the Dabblers, but I was to hear of them again. Act II was staged up at Scapa. I'd been transferred to a hospital ship, with a dislocated shoulder for X-ray, and as luck would have it the right-hand cot to mine was occupied by a lieu- tenant, RNVR, a fellow called Holster, who had been at old Edmed's school a year or two before my time. From him I learned a little more about the Dabblers. It seemed that they were boys who for some reason or other kept up a school tradition. Holster thought that they got out of the house by means of the big wistaria outside B dormitory, after leaving carefully constructed dummies in their beds. On the night in June when the Dabblers were due to appear it was considered bad form to stay awake too long and very unhealthy to ask too many questions, so that the iden- tity of the Dabblers remained a mystery. To the big and burly Holster there was nothing really mysterious about the thing; it was a schoolboys' lark and nothing more. An unsatisfactory act, you will agree, and one which fails to carry the story forward. But with the third act the drama begins to move. You see I had the good luck to meet one of the Dabblers in the flesh.

'Burlingham was badly shell-shocked in the war; a psychoanalyst took him in hand and he made a seemingly miraculous recovery. Then two years ago he had a partial relapse, and when I met him at Lady Byfleet's he was going up to town three times a week for special treatment from some unqualified West End practitioner, who seemed to be getting at the root of the trouble. There was something extraordinarily likeable about the man. He had a whimsical sense of humour that must have been his salvation, and with it was combined a capacity for intense indignation that one doesn't often meet with these days. We had a number of interesting talks together (part of his regime consisted of long cross-country walks, and he was glad enough of a companion) but the one I naturally remember was when in a tirade against English educational methods he mentioned Dr Edmed's name—"the head of a beastly little grammar school where I spent five of the most miserable years of my life."'

'"Three more than I did," I replied.

'"Good God!" he said, "fancy you being a product of that place!"

'"I was one of the producers," I answered. "I'm not proud of the fact; I usually keep it dark."

'"There was a lot too much kept dark about that

place," said Burlingham. It was the second time he had used the words. As he uttered them, "that place" sounded almost the equivalent of an unnamable hell. We talked for a time about the school, of Edmed's pomposity, of old Jacobson the porter—a man whose patient good humour shone alike on the just and on the unjust—of the rat hunts in the tithe barn on the last afternoons of term.

'"And now," I said at last, "tell me about the Dabblers."

'He turned round on me like a flash and burst out laughing, a high-pitched, nervous laugh that, remembering his condition, made me sorry I had introduced the subject.

'"How damnably funny!" he said. "The man I go to in town asked me the same question only a fortnight ago. I broke an oath in telling him, but I don't see why you shouldn't know as well. Not that there is anything to know; it's all a queer boyish nightmare without rhyme or reason. You see I was one of the Dabblers myself."

'It was a curious disjointed story that I got out of Burlingham. The Dabblers were a little society of five, sworn on solemn oath to secrecy. On a certain night in June, after warning had been given by their leader, they climbed out of the dormitories and met by the elm-tree in old Edmed's garden. A raid was made on the doctor's poultry run, and, having secured a fowl, they retired to the tithe barn, cut its throat, plucked and cleaned it, and then roasted it over a fire in a brazier while the rats looked on. The leader of the Dabblers produced sticks of incense; he lit his own from the fire, the others kindling theirs from his.

Then all moved in slow procession to the summer-house in the corner of the doctor's garden, singing as they went. There was no sense in the words they sang. They weren't English and they weren't Latin. Burlingham described them as reminding him of the refrain in the old nursery rhyme:

> There were three brothers over the sea,
> *Peri meri dixd domine.*
> They sent three presents unto me,
> *Petrum partrum paradisi tempore*
> *Peri meri dixi domine.*

' "And that was all?" I said to him.

' "Yes," he replied, "that was all there was to it; but—"

'I expected the but.

' "We were all of us frightened, horribly frightened. It was quite different from the ordinary schoolboy escapade. And yet there was fascination, too, in the fear. It was rather like," and here he laughed, "dragging a deep pool for the body of someone who had been drowned. You didn't know who it was, and you wondered what would turn up."

'I asked him a lot of questions but he hadn't anything very definite to tell us. The Dabblers were boys in the lower and middle forms and with the exception of the leader their membership of the fraternity was limited to two years. Quite a number of the boys, according to Burlingham, must have been Dabblers, but they never talked about it and no one, as far as he knew, had broken his oath. The leader in his time was called Tancred, the most unpopular boy in the school, despite the fact that he was their best athlete. He was expelled following an incident that took place in chapel. Burlingham didn't know what it was; he was away in the sick-room at the time, and the accounts, I gather, varied considerably.'

Harborough broke off to fill his pipe.

'Act IV will follow immediately,' he said.

'All this is very interesting,' observed Scott, 'but I'm afraid that if it's your object to curdle our blood you haven't quite succeeded. And if you hope to spring a surprise on us in Act IV we must disillusion you.' Freeman nodded assent.

'"Scott who Edgar Wallace read,"' he began. 'We're familiar nowadays with the whole bag of tricks. Black Mass is a certain winner; I put my money on him. Go on, Harborough.'

'You don't give a fellow half a chance, but I suppose you're right. Act IV takes place in the study of the Rev Montague Cuttler, vicar of St Mary Parbeloe, a former senior mathematics master, but before Edmed's time—a dear old boy, blind as a bat, and a Fellow of the Society of Antiquaries. He knew nothing about the Dabblers. He wouldn't. But he knew a very great deal about the past history of the school, when it wasn't a school but a monastery. He used to do a little quiet excavating in the vacations and had discovered what he believed to be the stone that marked the tomb of Abbot Polegate. The man, it appeared, had a bad reputation for dabbling in forbidden mysteries.'

'Hence the name Dabblers, I suppose,' said Scott.

'I'm not so sure,' Harborough answered. 'I think that more probably it's derived from *diabolos*. But, anyhow, from old Cuttler I gathered that the abbot's stone was where Edmed had placed his summer-house. Now doesn't it all illustrate my theory beauti-fully? I admit that there are no thrills in the story. There's nothing really supernatural about it. Only it does show the power of oral tradition when you think of a bastard form of the black mass surviving like this for hundreds of years under the very noses of the pedagogues.'

'It shows too,' said Freeman, 'what we have to suffer from incompetent headmasters. Now at the place I was telling you about where I've entered my boy—and I wish I could show you their workshops and art rooms—they've got a fellow who is—'

'What was the name of the school?' interrupted Harborough.

'Whitechurch Abbey.'

'And a fortnight ago, you say, two boys were expelled for a raid on a hen roost?'

'Yes.'

'Well, it's the same place that I've been talking about. The Dabblers were out.'

'Act V,' said Scott, 'and curtain. Harborough, you've got your thrill after all.'

*   *   *

WILLIAM HARVEY is remembered as a popular writer of creepy ghost stories and the author of a classic horror tale filmed and adapted for television, *The Beast with Five Fingers* (1928), in which a man is haunted by a disembodied hand. He was educated at Balliol College, Oxford and for some years worked at the Fircroft College near Birmingham. During the First World War, Harvey enlisted in the Navy and in 1918 he was awarded the Albert Medal for saving the life of another sailor trapped in the wrecked and flooded engine-room of a destroyer that was in danger of breaking in two. He suffered terrible internal injuries for his bravery and after the war lived quietly in Switzerland writing stories to make readers shiver such as 'August Heat', 'Across The Moors' and 'The Dabblers'. An admirer of his work, Maurice Richardson, said of this story about schoolboy occultists: 'It strikes me as a really original little fantasy—*all the more impressive on account of its essential possibility.*'

THE MAGIC OF FLYING

Jacqueline Wilson

*There are lots of amazing creatures to be found in the lore
of wizardry: traditional beasts like fire-breathing dragons
and huge serpents as well as more everyday animals including black cats, hell hounds and magic frogs who may, or
may not, turn into prince's when they are kissed. In this
next story we meet perhaps the most commonplace of all
magical creatures, a toad, and the little girl Rebecca, who
befriends him. Now, Rebecca knows about witchcraft because
her dad has explained the history of it to her. She was a bit
upset, though, over his story of a pond near their home
where long ago women who were suspected of being witches
were thrown into the deep water. If they floated, they were
guilty of evil things, dad said; if they did not, of course they
drowned. It didn't seem at all fair to Rebecca. Then she met
a huge toad who lived in the witch's pond. But this is no
ordinary toad: he is hundreds of years old, can talk and
work the most amazing magic. His name is Glubbslyme and
he was the familiar of a seventeenth-century witch, also
called Rebecca Cockgoldde, who had been tortured and
drowned in the pond. Our Rebecca is enchanted by the toad
and begs him to teach her magic. In particular, how to
fly . . .*

*   *   *

'Will you teach me how to fly?' Rebecca asked the toad.

Glubbslyme swung his legs and sighed.

'I do not care for flying,' he said. 'I suffer from vertigo.'

'What's that?' said Rebecca, wondering if it might be a dread seventeenth-century disease.

But it was only dizziness.

'Only!' said Glubbslyme, closing his eyes. 'Once I fell from the broomstick when we did fly to attend a Great Sabbat and I hurtled downwards like a hawk. I was certain I would spatter the ground with my chill blood but my dear Rebecca swooped after me and rescued me just in time.'

'I won't let you fall, Glubbslyme, I promise. Oh please, I'd give anything to be able to fly. Please. *Please.*'

Glubbslyme sighed irritably.

'Very well. One *very* brief flying lesson. First you will need to concoct a flying ointment. My Rebecca used the strongest ointment possible because she ventured far and wide. A weaker lotion will be sufficient for your purposes. Now, as to ingredients. Of course Rebecca varied hers according to her needs. When we did fly over three counties on All Hallow's Eve she did use a goose grease base and added eagle's claw and albatross eye, bat's blood and the gore from a dangling man. I do not suppose there is a gibbet nearby, child?'

'What's a gibbet?'

'It is the post on which malefactors are hung.'

'We don't have them nowadays,' said Rebecca gratefully.

Glubbslyme tutted. 'Well, I daresay we can make do with eagle, albatross and bat.'

'I don't think that's going to be possible either,' said Rebecca. 'I'm sure I couldn't catch an eagle or an albatross and I'm scared of bats.'

'You cannot fly without an aerial ointment,' said Glubbslyme impatiently. He peered out of the kitchen window at the birds on the fence. 'Suppose we keep things simple? Kindly catch six sparrows.'

'I'm not extracting any eyes or beaks or claws,' said Rebecca firmly. 'And besides, I'd get reported to the RSPCA'

She made do with two sparrow feathers, a dead bumble bee and the wing of one of Glubbslyme's snack dragonflies. She made a thick white paste with washing powder (because it was called Ariel), chopped the feathers, bee and wing into tiny pieces, and added them to the mixture.

'It looks rather disgusting,' she said. 'It was a very dead bee.'

'Beggars cannot be choosers,' said Glubbslyme. 'Now bring me your broomstick and we will anoint ourselves with your inferior ointment.'

There was a further problem.

'I haven't got a broomstick,' said Rebecca.

'No broomstick,' said Glubbslyme. 'Might I enquire how you sweep your floors?'

Rebecca went to the cupboard and brought out the vacuum cleaner and the dustpan and brush. Glubbslyme did not understand the vacuum cleaner so she switched it on and showed him. He shrieked and leaped for the safety of the kitchen sink.

'It's all right, Glubbslyme, there's nothing to be

frightened of, I promise,' said Rebecca, switching off. 'I used to be scared of the vacuum too—but that was just when I was a little baby.'

'I do not think you were ever little enough to be sucked up into that dreadful nozzle,' said Glubbslyme, shuddering. 'Kindly banish it back into its cupboard. And we will not require the child's broom either. It might prove an adequate steed for such as myself but it will not bear your great weight.'

Rebecca was hurt. She was perhaps a bit plumper than Sarah and skinny old Mandy but she really wasn't *fat.*

'What *can* we use then?' she asked, chucking the vacuum and brush back in the cupboard.

Glubbslyme was peering into its depths.

'What is the long pied stick in the corner?' he asked.

Rebecca realized he meant Dad's red and yellow umbrella.

'It will suffice,' said Glubbslyme. 'Apply the ointment. We are about to learn how to fly.'

Rebecca stuck her fingers into her unpleasant Ariel ointment and smeared a little on her arms and legs. She tried to avoid the little black bits in case they were the bee. The ointment felt uncomfortably itchy. She hoped she wouldn't get a rash, she had very sensitive skin.

'And me,' commanded Glubbslyme.

She smeared the ointment over his odd warty back. Glubbslyme certainly did not appear to have sensitive skin but when she worked round his tummy he grinned foolishly and doubled up.

'Desist!' he gasped. 'I am extremely ticklish.'

Rebecca became very giggly too, in nervous excitement. Glubbslyme told her to mount her steed.
Rebecca straddled the umbrella, feeling rather a fool.
She remembered long-ago games of hobby-horse,
and wondered if she should give the umbrella an
encouraging click of the teeth.

'Aren't you getting on too?' she asked Glubbslyme.

'Not unless it is absolutely necessary,' said
Glubbslyme. 'Now concentrate, child. *Will* the pied
stick up into the ether.'

Rebecca willed as hard as she could, her eyes
squeezed shut with effort. Nothing at all happened.
She stayed standing on the unmopped kitchen floor,
straddling the umbrella.

'Try harder! Concentrate,' said Glubbslyme.

Rebecca tried. She concentrated until she thought
her brain would burst but still nothing happened.
Glubbslyme suggested another application of ointment, so she rubbed until her arms and legs were
coated in white, and she dabbed more ointment on
her face and even up under her T-shirt. She felt horribly stiff and sticky and it made no difference what-
soever.

'You seem to have no rudimentary aptitude whatso-
ever,' Glubbslyme grumbled. 'I will have to join you
after all.'

He hopped up gingerly behind her. The umbrella
immediately twitched.

'Oh mercy, my stomach,' Glubbslyme moaned.

'It moved, Glubbslyme! I felt it move,' Rebecca
cried excitedly.

'I am in fear that my syrup pottage will move too,'
said Glubbslyme. 'Are you certain you wish to fly?'

'Oh I do, I do!'

'So be it,' Glubbslyme sighed. 'Give the magical command.'

Rebecca gabbled seven Glubbslymes while his eyes revolved one, two, three, four, five, six, seven times. The umbrella twitched again, and then it jerked violently upwards, catching Rebecca off balance so that she shot down the umbrella, severely squashing Glubbslyme. There was one confused shrieking second when they were all actually airborne but then they clattered separately on to the kitchen floor. The umbrella lay quietly where it fell. Glubbslyme did not lie quietly. He hopped up and down, croaking furiously, rubbing his sore arm and bumped head. Rebecca had twisted her ankle and bumped her own head on the edge of the kitchen table but she did not dare complain. She concentrated on soothing Glubbslyme, which wasn't easy.

'You clumsy dim-witted dolt,' he hissed.

'I know, and I'm ever so sorry, Glubbslyme, really I am. I swear I won't squash you next time. It was just it all happened so quickly it took me by surprise. Please let's have another go. You sit in front of me to be on the safe side.'

'There is no safe side where you are concerned,' said Glubbslyme, but he hopped over to the umbrella and settled himself upon it, crouching right up at the handle. Rebecca followed him and sat on the umbrella, clutching it as tightly as she could with her hands, and her knees too for good measure. She chanted seven Glubbslymes. Glubbslyme wearily revolved his eyes one, two, three, four, five, six, seven times and the umbrella quivered into action. It rose in the air—and Rebecca and Glubbslyme rose too. They reached the level of the kitchen table.

'We're doing it, we're doing it!' Rebecca shouted, and she was so excited she lost all her common sense and waved her legs wildly to convince herself she was actually up off the ground. She did not stay up off the ground for very long. Waving her legs made the umbrella tilt sideways. It stabbed at the kitchen shelves, sweeping the biscuit tin onto the floor, and the impact made it twist and whirl. Rebecca and Glubbslyme twisted and whirled too and rapidly returned to the kitchen floor. The umbrella stayed spinning in mid-air for a few seconds as if it hadn't noticed they were missing, but then it tumbled down and landed with a thwack against the door frame, chipping off a large flake of paint.

'Oh help,' said Rebecca wearily.

Glubbslyme said nothing at all for several seconds. He lay flat on his back, twitching.

'Glubbslyme? You are all right, aren't you?' Rebecca enquired anxiously.

'I am exceeding all *wrong*,' said Glubbslyme. He struggled to his feet and brushed biscuit crumbs from his body. He nibbled one absent-mindedly, and then started serious munching. 'We will abandon this flying foolery forthwith. Perhaps you relish the idea of pain and confusion and indignity. I do not.'

'But I can't give up now, not when I'm just getting the hang of it,' said Rebecca.

'You are "getting the hang" of falling, not flying,' said Glubbslyme.

'Can't we have a few more goes, please? I really did do it. I was right up in the air.'

Glubbslyme sighed. Rebecca picked up some bigger bits of biscuit to persuade him. She'd have to sweep the kitchen floor properly and see if there was any way she could stick the piece of paint-flake back on to the door frame but she wasn't going to bother about that now.

There wasn't much point in bothering. On her next flight she knocked the cornflake packet off the shelf too, and the flight after that she managed to fly smack into the wall, and the point of Dad's umbrella chipped a great chunk out of the plaster. That really did alarm her and she tried doing a temporary repair with the last of the Ariel ointment, which proved totally ineffective.

'What's Dad going to say?' she whispered—but the feeling of flying had been so wonderful she soon stopped worrying. She decided she simply didn't have room enough in the kitchen, so she persuaded Glubbslyme to perch on the umbrella at the top of the stairs.

It was a sensible idea. Rebecca could kick off and actually aim the umbrella. They flew from the top of the stairs to the bottom, zig-zagging a little and landing in a heap in the hall, but it was proper flight for all that.

'Isn't it fantastic!' said Rebecca, jumping up and down with excitement. 'It's heaps and heaps better than riding a bike or going down a slide.'

'Desist,' Glubbslyme groaned. 'There is no need to bounce like a ball in a cup. I feel giddy enough as it is without your crazy bobbing up and down.'

'Oh Glubbslyme, you can't possibly be feeling

giddy when we flew such a little way! Come on, let's do it again. And again and again and again.'

'You do it. Again and again. I will lie here and close my eyes until the world stops spinning,' groaned Glubbslyme.

Rebecca wondered if she really could do it by herself. She did seem to have got the knack now. She decided to give it a try. She wisely did not climb to the top of the stairs. She straddled the umbrella and launched herself into the air three steps from the bottom. It was just as well. She landed very quickly indeed on both knees and her chin. She lay where she was with her bottom sticking up in the air, wondering whether her teeth were still attached. She ran her tongue over them gingerly but they all seemed to be in place. Then she wondered if her jaw had dislocated, but when she sat up she found she could move it easily if painfully.

'Why are you grimacing so terribly?' Glubbslyme enquired. 'Are you having a seizure?'

'No, of course not. I'm sort of putting my face back into place because it got banged a bit. Glubbslyme, I can't fly at all without you.'

'I am aware of that,' said Glubbslyme.

'So will you do it with me? Just *once* more?'

Glubbslyme reluctantly complied. They flew from the top of the stairs to the bottom. Apart from one bump on the bannisters it was a perfect flight. Rebecca tried for another once more. And then another. She was starting to be able to steer properly now, and this time she even managed a decorous landing, feet first.

'I can do it, I can do it!' she yelled triumphantly.

'I?' said Glubbslyme.

'We. You. Oh Glubbslyme, no wonder they called you great. You really are. You're the most magical toad ever. I'm so proud and pleased that you're my familiar!'

*   *   *

JACQUELINE WILSON has been described by *Time* magazine as 'Britain's second favourite living children's author' after J. K. Rowling. She has written about seventy books in all and sold over 4 million copies, not to mention winning numerous honours including the Children's Book Award, the Smarties Prize and being short-listed several times for the Carnegie Medal. She was born in Somerset and her early career was in magazines, in particular on the teen magazine, *Jackie*, which was named after her. She recalls, 'My ambitions were to be published, get a few nice reviews and maybe a prize. But never, ever did I think there would be best-selling books.' Wilson's ability to write about young girls—all resourceful, feisty and with a sense of humour—in every kind of situation from a broken home to a brush with the supernatural rapidly made her a great favourite. Among the scariest of her books have been *The Monster in the Cupboard* (1986), the series about Stevie Day including *Stevie Day, Supersleuth* (1987) and *Stevie Day, Vampire* (1988), and the creepy adventures of *The Werepuppy* (1991). Jacqueline Wilson regularly visits schools—'Good for my street cred,' she claims—runs classes for children in creative writing and says she just *loves* reading—she apparently has over 10,000 books in her own collection at home!

CHINESE PUZZLE

John Wyndham

Dragons are undoubtedly the most popular creatures in the history of wizardry and stories about them can be found from the time of Merlin right up to the present day. There are supposed to be various species around the world, differing from the dangerous kind in Britain and Europe as slain by St George to the benevolent sort mentioned in Chinese mythology which date back 3,000 years and more. Famous fictional dragons have included the evil Smaug in Tolkien's Lord of the Rings (1954), *the beautiful and superior types found in Ursula Le Guin's* Wizard of Earthsea *series in the 1960s and 1970s, and the pairing of a large and malevolent dragon with a bunch of little pet dragons prone to hiccups in Terry Pratchett's comical* Discworld *novel,* Guards! Guards! (1989). *They feature largely in the Harry Potter stories, too, and Ron Weasley, Harry's closest friend, is a great expert on them. When, for example, Harry says that there aren't any wild dragons in Britain any more, Ron insists, 'Of course there are— Common Welsh Green and Hebridean Blacks'. They are also very much a part of the Hogwarts legend: the school motto,* Draco Dormiens Nunquam Titillandus, *translates as 'Never Tickle a Sleeping Dragon' and among the school textbooks can be found* Dragon Species of Great Britain and Ireland *and* From Egg to Inferno: A Dragon-Keeper's Guide. *(J. K. Rowling has even been asked what you should feed a baby dragon on and thinks the best thing is a mixture of chicken blood and brandy!) In this next story, Dafyyd sends his mum and dad in Wales a strange egg from China. No one in Llangolwgoch is quite sure what it is until the morning the parents find the shell broken and a lizard-like creature with goggling red eyes and a long, greeny-blue tail staring up at them. When the creature suddenly snorts two jets of flame and a puff of smoke they have a very good idea* indeed . . .

*　　*　　*

The parcel, waiting provocatively on the dresser, was the first thing that Hwyl noticed when he got in from work.

'From Dai, is it?' he inquired of his wife.

'Yes, indeed. Japanese the stamps are,' she told him.

He went across to examine it. It was the shape a small hatbox might be, about ten inches each way, perhaps. The address: Mr & Mrs Hwyl Hughes, Ty Derwen, Llynllawn, Llangolwgcoch, Brecknockshire, S. Wales, was lettered carefully, for the clear understanding of foreigners. The other label, also hand-lettered, but in red, was quite clear, too. It said: EGGS—Fragile—With great CARE.

'There is funny to send eggs so far,' Hwyl said. 'Plenty of eggs we are having. Might be chocolate eggs, I think?'

'Come you to your tea, man,' Bronwen told him. 'All day I have been looking at that old parcel, and a little longer it can wait now.'

Hwyl sat down at the table and began his meal.

From time to time, however, his eyes strayed again to the parcel.

'If it is real eggs they are, careful you should be,' he remarked. 'Reading in a book I was once how in China they keep eggs for years. Bury them in the earth, they do, for a delicacy. There is strange for you, now. Queer they are in China, and not like Wales, at all.'

Bronwen contented herself with saying that perhaps Japan was not like China, either.

When the meal had been finished and cleared, the parcel was transferred to the table. Hwyl snipped the string and pulled off the brown paper. Within was a tin box which, when the sticky tape holding its lid had been removed, proved to be full to the brim with sawdust. Mrs Hughes fetched a sheet of newspaper, and prudently covered the table-top. Hwyl dug his fingers into the sawdust.

'Something there, there is,' he announced.

'There is stupid you are. Of course there is something there, Bronwen said, slapping his hand out of the way.

She trickled some of the sawdust out on to the newspaper, and then felt inside the box herself. Whatever it was, it felt much too large for an egg. She poured out more sawdust and felt again. This time, her fingers encountered a piece of paper. She pulled it out and laid it on the table; a letter in Dafydd's handwriting. Then she put in her hand once more, got her fingers under the object, and lifted it gently out.

'Well, indeed! Look at that now! Did you ever?' she exclaimed. 'Eggs, he was saying, is it?'

They both regarded it with astonishment for some moments.

'So big it is. Queer, too,' said Hwyl, at last.

'What kind of bird to lay such an egg?' said Bronwen.

'Ostrich, perhaps?' suggested Hwyl.

But Bronwen shook her head. She had once seen an ostrich's egg in a museum, and remembered it well enough to know that it had little in common with this. The ostrich's egg had been a little smaller, with a dull, sallow-looking, slightly-dimpled surface. This was smooth and shiny, and by no means had the same dead look: it had a lustre to it, a nacreous kind of beauty.

'A pearl, could it be?' she said, in an awed voice.

'There is silly you are,' said her husband. 'From an oyster as big as Llangolwgcoch Town Hall, you are thinking?'

He burrowed into the tin again, but 'Eggs', it seemed, had been a manner of speaking: there was no other, nor room for one.

Bronwen put some of the sawdust into one of her best vegetable-dishes, and bedded the egg carefully on top of it. Then they sat down to read their son's letter:

S. S. Tudor Maid,
Kobe.

Dear Mam and Dad,

I expect you will be surprised about the enclosed I was too. It is a funny looking thing I expect they have funny birds in China after all they have Pandas so why not. We found a small sampan about a hundred miles off the China coast that had bust its mast and should never have tried and all except two of them were dead they are all dead now. But one of them that wasn't dead then was holding this egg-thing all wrapped up in a padded coat like it was a baby only I didn't know it was an egg then not till later. One of them died coming aboard but this other one lasted two days longer in spite of all I could do for him which was my best. I was sorry nobody here can speak Chinese because he was a nice little chap and lonely and knew he was a goner but there it is. And when he saw it was nearly all up he gave me this egg and talked very faint but I'd not have understood anyway. All I could do was take it and hold it careful the way he had and tell him I'd look after it which he couldn't understand either. Then he said something else and looked very worried and died poor chap.

So here it is. I know it is an egg because I took him a boiled egg once he pointed to both of them to show me but nobody on board knows what kind of egg. But seeing I promised him I'd keep it safe I am sending it to you to keep for me as this ship is no place to keep anything safe anyway and hope it doesn't get cracked on the way too.

Hoping this finds you as it leaves me and love to all and you special.

Dai.

'Well, there is strange for you, now,' said Mrs Hughes, as she finished reading. 'And *looking* like an egg it is, indeed—the shape of it,' she conceded. 'But the colours are not. There is pretty they are. Like you see when oil is on the road in the rain. But never an egg like that have I seen in my life. Flat the colour is on eggs, and not to shine.'

Hwyl went on looking at it thoughtfully.

'Yes. There is beautiful,' he agreed, 'but what use?'

'Use, is it, indeed!' said his wife. 'A trust, it is, and sacred, too. Dying the poor man was, and our Dai gave him his word. I am thinking of how we will keep it safe for him till he will be back, now.'

They both contemplated the egg awhile.

'Very far away, China is,' Bronwen remarked, obscurely.

Several days passed, however, before the egg was removed from display on the dresser. Word quickly went round the valley about it, and the callers would have felt slighted had they been unable to see it. Bronwen felt that continually getting it out and putting it away again would be more hazardous than leaving it on exhibition.

Almost everyone found the sight of it rewarding. Idris Bowen who lived three houses away was practically alone in his divergent view.

'The shape of an egg, it has,' he allowed. 'But careful you should be, Mrs Hughes. A fertility symbol it is, I am thinking, and stolen, too, likely.'

'Mr Bowen—' began Bronwen, indignantly.

'Oh, by the men in that boat, Mrs Hughes. Refugees from China they would be, see. Traitors to the Chinese people. And running away with all they could carry, before the glorious army of the workers and peasants could catch them, too. Always the same, it is, as you will be seeing when the revolution comes to Wales.'

'Oh, dear, dear! There is funny you are, Mr Bowen. Propaganda you will make out of an old boot, I think,' said Bronwen.

Idris Bowen frowned.

'Funny, I am not, Mrs Hughes. And propaganda there is in an honest boot, too,' he told her as he left with dignity.

By the end of a week practically everyone in the village had seen the egg and been told no, Mrs Hughes did not know what kind of a creature had laid it, and the time seemed to have come to store it away safely against Dafydd's return. There were not many places in the house where she could feel sure that it would rest undisturbed, but, on consideration, the airing-cupboard seemed as likely as any, so she put it back on what sawdust was left in the tin, and stowed it in there.

It remained there for a month, out of sight, and pretty much out of mind until a day when Hwyl returning from work discovered his wife sitting at the table with a disconsolate expression on her face, and a bandage on her finger. She looked relieved to see him.

'Hatched, it is,' she observed.

The blankness of Hwyl's expression was irritating to one who had had a single subject on her mind all day.

'Dai's egg,' she explained. 'Hatched out, it is, I am telling you.'

'Well, there is a thing for you, now!' said Hwyl. 'A nice little chicken is it?'

'A chicken it is not, at all. A monster, indeed, and biting me it is, too.' She held out her bandaged finger.

She explained that this morning she had gone to the airing-cupboard to take out a clean towel, and as she put her hand in, something had nipped her finger, painfully. At first she had thought that it might be a rat that had somehow got in from the yard, but then she had noticed that the lid was off the tin, and the shell of the egg there was all broken to pieces.

'How is it to see?' Hwyl asked.

Bronwen admitted that she had not seen it well. She had had a glimpse of a long, greeny-blue tail protruding from behind a pile of sheets, and then it had looked at her over the top of them, glaring at her from red eyes. On that, it had seemed to her more the kind of a job a man should deal with, so she had slammed the door, and gone to bandage her finger.

'Still there, then, is it?' said Hwyl.

She nodded.

'Right now. Have a look at it, we will, now then,' he said, decisively.

He started to leave the room, but on second thoughts turned back to collect a pair of heavy working-gloves. Bronwen did not offer to accompany him.

Presently there was a scuffle of his feet, an exclamation or two, then his tread descending the stairs. He came in, shutting the door behind him with his foot. He set the creature he was carrying down on the table, and for some seconds it crouched there, blinking, but otherwise unmoving.

'Scared, he was, I think,' Hwyl remarked.

In the body, the creature bore some resemblance to a lizard—a large lizard, over a foot long. The scales of its skin, however, were much bigger, and some of them curled up and stood out here and there, in a fin-like manner. And the head was quite unlike a lizard's, being much rounder, with a wide mouth, broad nostrils, and, overall, a slightly pushed-in effect, in which were set a pair of goggling red eyes. About the neck, and also making a kind of mane, were curious, streamer-like attachments with the suggestion of locks of hair which had permanently cohered. The colour was mainly green, shot with blue, and having a metallic shine to it, but there were brilliant red markings about the head and in the lower parts of the locks. There were touches of red, too, where the legs joined the body, and on the feet, where the toes finished in sharp yellow claws. Altogether, a surprisingly vivid and exotic creature.

It eyed Bronwen Hughes for a moment, turned a baleful look on Hwyl, and then started to run about the table-top, looking for a way off. The Hughes' watched it for a moment or two, and then regarded one another.

'Well, there is nasty for you, indeed,' observed Bronwen.

'Nasty it may be. But beautiful it is, too, look,' said Hwyl.

'Ugly old face to have,' Bronwen remarked.

'Yes. indeed. But fine colours, too, see. Glorious, they are, like technicolor, I am thinking,' Hwyl said.

The creature appeared to have half a mind to leap from the table. Hwyl leaned forward and caught hold of it. It wriggled, and tried to get its head round to bite him, but discovered he was holding it too near the neck for that. It paused in its struggles. Then, suddenly, it snorted. Two jets of flame and a puff of smoke came from its nostrils. Hwyl dropped it abruptly, partly from alarm, but more from surprise. Bronwen gave a squeal, and climbed hastily on to her chair.

The creature itself seemed a trifle astonished. For a few seconds it stood turning its head and waving the sinuous tail that was quite as long as its body. Then it scuttled across to the hearthrug, and curled itself up in front of the fire.

'By dammo! There was a thing for you!' Hwyl exclaimed, regarding it a trifle nervously. 'Fire there was with it, I think. I will like to understand that, now.'

'Fire indeed, and smoke, too,' Bronwen agreed. 'There is shocking it was, and not natural, at all.'

She looked uncertainly at the creature. It had so obviously settled itself for a nap that she risked stepping down from the chair, but she kept on watching it, ready to jump again if it should move. Then:

'Never did I think I will see one of those. And not sure it is right to have in the house, either,' she said. 'What is it you are meaning, now?' Hwyl asked, puzzled. 'Why, a dragon, indeed.' Bronwen told him.

Hwyl stared at her.

'Dragon!' he exclaimed. 'There is foolish—' Then he stopped. He looked at it again, and then down at the place where the flame had scorched his glove. 'No, by dammo!' he said. 'Right, you. A dragon it is, I believe.'

They both regarded it with some apprehension.

'Glad, I am, not to live in China,' observed Bronwen.

Those who were privileged to see the creature during the next day' or two supported almost to a man the theory that it was a dragon. This, they established by poking sticks through the wire-netting of the hutch that Hwyl had made for it until it obliged with a resentful huff of flame. Even Mr Jones, the Chapel, did not doubt its authenticity, though on the propriety of its presence in his community he preferred to reserve judgement for the present.

After a short time, however, Bronwen Hughes put an end to the practice of poking it. For one thing, she felt responsible to Dai for its well-being; for another, it was beginning to develop an irritable disposition, and a liability to emit flame without cause; for yet another, and although Mr Jones's decision on whether it could be considered as one of God's creatures or not was still pending, she felt that in the meantime it deserved equal rights with other dumb animals. So she put a card on the hutch saying: PLEASE NOT TO TEASE, and most of the time was there to see that it was heeded.

Almost all Llynllawn, and quite a few people from Llangolwgcoch, too, came to see it. Sometimes they would stand for an hour or more, hoping to see it huff. If it did, they went off satisfied that it was a dragon; but if it maintained a contented, non-fire-breathing mood, they went and told their friends that it was really no more than a little old lizard, though big, mind you.

Idris Bowen was an exception to both categories. It was not until his third visit that he was privileged to see it snort, but even then he remained unconvinced.

'Unusual, it is, yes,' he admitted. 'But a dragon it is not. Look you at the dragon of Wales, or the dragon of St George, now. To huff fire is something, I grant you, but wings, too, a dragon must be having, or a dragon he is not.'

But that was the kind of cavilling that could be expected from Idris, and disregarded.

After ten days or so of crowded evenings, however, interest slackened. Once one had seen the dragon and exclaimed over the brilliance of its colouring, there was little to add, beyond being glad that it was in the Hughes' house rather than one's own, and wondering how big it would eventually grow. For, really, it did not do much but sit and blink, and perhaps give a little huff of flame if you were lucky. So, presently, the Hughes' home became more their own again.

And, no longer pestered by visitors, the dragon showed an equable disposition. It never huffed at Bronwen, and seldom at Hwyl. Bronwen's first feeling of antagonism passed quickly, and she found herself growing attached to it. She fed it, and looked after it, and found that on a diet consisting chiefly of minced horseflesh and dog-biscuits it grew with astonishing speed. Most of the time, she let it run free in the room. To quieten the misgivings of callers she would explain:

'Friendly, he is, and pretty ways he has with him, if there is not teasing. Sorry for him, I am, too, for bad it is to be an only child, and an orphan worse still. And less than an orphan, he is, see. Nothing of his own sort he is knowing, nor likely, either. So very lonely he is being, poor thing, I think.'

But, inevitably, there came an evening when Hwyl, looking thoughtfully at the dragon, remarked:

'Outside you, son. There is too big for the house you are getting, see.'

Bronwen was surprised to find how unwilling she felt about that.

'Very good and quiet, he is,' she said. 'There is clever he is to tuck his tail away not to trip people, too. And clean with the house he is, also, and no trouble. Always out to the yard at proper times. Right as clockwork.'

'Behaving well, he is, indeed,' Hwyl agreed. 'But growing so fast, now. More room he will be needing, see. A fine hutch for him in the yard, and with a run to it, I think.'

The advisability of that was demonstrated a week later when Bronwen came down one morning to find the end of the wooden hutch charred away, the carpet and rug smouldering, and the dragon comfortably curled up in Hwyl's easy chair.

'Settled, it is, and lucky indeed not to burn in our bed. Out you,' Hwyl told the dragon. 'A fine thing to burn a man's house for him, and not grateful, either. For shame, I am telling you.'

The insurance man who came to inspect the damage thought similarly.

'Notified, you should have,' he told Bronwen. 'A fire-risk, he is, you see.'

Bronwen protested that the policy made no mention of dragons.

'No, indeed,' the man admitted, 'but a normal hazard he is not, either. Inquire, I will, from Head Office how it is, see. But better to turn him out before more trouble, and thankful, too.'

So, a couple of days later, the dragon was occupying a larger hutch, constructed of asbestos sheets, in the yard. There was a wire-netted run in front of it, but most of the time Bronwen locked the gate, and left the back-door of the house open so that he could come and go as he liked. In the morning he would trot in, and help Bronwen by huffing the kitchen fire into a blaze, but apart from that he had learnt not to huff in the house. The only times he was any bother to anyone were the occasions when he set his straw on fire in the night so that the neighbours got up to see if the house was burning, and were some-what short about it the next day.

Hwyl kept a careful account of the cost of feeding him, and hoped that it was not running into more than Dai would be willing to pay. Otherwise, his only worries were his failure to find a cheap, non-inflammable bedding-stuff, and speculation on how big the dragon was likely to grow before Dai should return to take him off his hands. Very likely all would have gone smoothly until that happened, but for the unpleasantness with Idris Bowen.

The trouble which blew up unexpectedly one evening was really of Idris' own finding. Hwyl had finished his meal, and was peacefully enjoying the last of the day beside his door, when Idris happened along, leading his whippet on a string.

'Oh, hullo you, Idris,' Hwyl greeted him, amiably.

'Hullo you, Hwyl,' said Idris. 'And how is that phoney dragon of yours, now then?'

'Phoney, is it, you are saying?' repeated Hwyl, indig-nantly.

Wings, a dragon is wanting, to be a dragon,' Idris insisted, firmly.

'Wings to hell, man! Come you and look at him now then, and please to tell me what he is if he is no dragon.'

He waved Idris into the house, and led him through

into the yard. The dragon, reclining in its wired run, opened an eye at them, and closed it again.

Idris had not seen it since it was lately out of the egg. Its growth impressed him.

'There is big he is now,' he conceded. 'Fine the colours of him, and fancy, too. But still no wings to him; so a dragon he is not.'

'What then is it he is?' demanded Hwyl. 'Tell me that.'

How Idris would have replied to this difficult question was never to be known, for at that moment the whippet jerked its string free from his fingers, and dashed, barking, at the wire-netting. The dragon was startled out of its snooze. It sat up suddenly, and snorted with surprise. There was a yelp from the whippet which bounded into the air, and then set off round and round the yard, howling. At last Idris managed to corner it and pick it up. All down the right side its hair had been scorched off, making it look very peculiar. Idris' eyebrows lowered.

'Trouble you want, is it? And trouble you will be having, by God!' he said.

He put the whippet down again, and began to take off his coat.

It was not clear whether he had addressed, and meant to fight, Hwyl or the dragon, but either intention was forestalled by Mrs Hughes coming to investigate the yelping.

'Oh! Teasing the dragon, is it!' she said. 'There is shameful, indeed. A lamb the dragon is, as people know well. But not to tease. It is wicked you are, Idris Bowen, and to fight does not make right, either. Go you from here, now then.'

Idris began to protest, but Bronwen shook her head and set her mouth.

'Not listening to you, I am, see. A fine brave man, to tease a helpless dragon. Not for weeks now has the dragon huffed. So you go, and quick.'

Idris glowered. He hesitated, and pulled on his jacket again. He collected his whippet, and held it in his arms. After a final disparaging glance at the dragon, he turned.

'Law I will have of you,' he announced ominously, as he left.

Nothing more, however, was heard of legal action. It seemed as if Idris had either changed his mind or been advised against it, and that the whole thing would blow over. But three weeks later was the night of the Union Branch Meeting.

It had been a dull meeting, devoted chiefly to passing a number of resolutions suggested to it by its headquarters, as a matter of course. Then, just at the end, when there did not seem to be any other business, Idris Bowen rose.

'Stay you!' said the chairman to those who were preparing to leave, and he invited Idris to speak.

Idris waited for persons who were half-in and half-out of their overcoats to subside, then:

'Comrades—' he began.

There was immediate uproar. Through the mingled approbation and cries of 'Order' and 'Withdraw' the chairman smote energetically with his gavel until quiet was restored.

'Tendentious, that is,' he reproved Idris. 'Please to speak half-way, and in good order.'

Idris began again:

'Fellow-workers. Sorry indeed, I am, to have to tell you of a discovery I am making. A matter of disloyalty, I am telling you: grave disloyalty to good friends and com—and fellow workers, see.' He paused, and went on:

'Now, every one of you is knowing of Hwyl Hughes' dragon, is it? Seen him for yourselves you have likely, too. Seen him myself, I have, and saying he was no dragon. But now then, I am telling you, wrong I was, wrong, indeed. A dragon he is, and not to doubt, though no wings.

'I am reading in the Encyclopædia in Merthyr Public Library about two kinds of dragons, see. Wings the European dragon has, indeed. But wings the Oriental dragon has not. So apologizing now to Mr Hughes, I am, and sorry.'

A certain restiveness becoming apparent in the audience was quelled by a change in his tone.

'*But*—' he went on, 'but another thing, too, I am reading there, and troubled inside myself with it, I am. I will tell you. Have you looked at the feet of this dragon, is it? Claws there is, yes, and nasty, too. But how many, I am asking you? And five, I am telling you. Five with each foot.' He paused dramatically, and shook his head. 'Bad, is that, bad, indeed. For, look you, Chinese a five-toed dragon is, yes—but five-toed is not a Republican dragon, five-toed is not a People's dragon; five-toed is an *Imperial* dragon, see. A symbol, it is, of the oppression of Chinese workers and peasants. And shocking to think that in our village we are keeping such an emblem. What is it that the free people of China will be saying of

Llynllawn when they will hear of this, I am asking? What is it Mao Tse Tung, a glorious leader of the heroic Chinese people in their magnificent fight for peace, will be thinking of South Wales and this imperialist dragon—?' he was continuing, when difference of view in the audience submerged his voice.

Again the chairman called the meeting to order. He offered Hwyl the opportunity to reply, and after the situation had been briefly explained, the dragon was, on a show of hands, acquitted of political implication by all but Idris' doctrinaire faction, and the meeting broke up.

Hwyl told Bronwen about it when he got home.

'No surprise there,' she said. 'Jones the Post is telling me, telegraphing Idris has been.'

'Telegraphing?' inquired Hwyl.

'Yes, indeed. Asking the *Daily Worker*, in London, how is the party-line on imperialist dragons, he was. But no answer yet, though.'

A few mornings later the Hugheses' were awakened by a hammering on their door. Hwyl went to the window and found Idris below. He asked what the matter was.

'Come you down here, and I will show you,' Idris told him.

After some argument. Hwyl descended. Idris led the way round to the back of his own house, and pointed.

'Look you there, now,' he said.

The door of Idris' henhouse was hanging by one hinge. The remains of two chickens lay close by.

A large quantity of feathers was blowing about the yard.

Hwyl looked at the henhouse more closely. Several deep-raked scores stood out white on the creosoted wood. In other places there were darker smears where the wood seemed to have been scorched. Silently Idris pointed to the ground. There were marks of sharp claws, but no imprint of a whole foot.

'There is bad. Foxes is it?' inquired Hwyl.

Idris choked slightly.

'Foxes, you are saying. Foxes, indeed! What will it be but your dragon? And the police to know it, too.'

Hwyl shook his head.

'No,' he said.

'Oh,' said Idris. 'A liar, I am, is it? I will have the guts from you, Hwyl Hughes, smoking hot, too, and glad to do it.'

'You talk too easy, man,' Hwyl told him. 'Only how the dragon is still fast in his hutch, I am saying. Come you now, and see.'

They went back to Hwyl's house. The dragon was in his hutch, sure enough, and the door of it was fastened with a peg. Furthermore, as Hwyl pointed out, even if he had left it during the night, he could not have reached Idris' yard without leaving scratches and traces on the way, and there were none to be found.

They finally parted in a state of armistice. Idris was by no means convinced, but he was unable to get round the facts, and not at all impressed with Hwyl's suggestion that a practical joker could have produced the effect on the henhouse with a strong nail and a blow-torch.

Hwyl went upstairs again to finish dressing.

'There is funny it is, all the same,' he observed to Bronwen. 'Not seeing, that Idris was, but scorched the peg is, on the *outside* of the hutch. And how should that be, I wonder?'

'Huffed four times in the night the dragon has, five, perhaps,' Bronwen said. 'Growling, he is, too, and banging that old hutch about. Never have I heard him like that before.'

'There is queer,' Hwyl said, frowning. 'But never out of his hutch, and that to swear to.'

Two nights later Hwyl was awakened by Bronwen shaking his shoulder.

'Listen, now then,' she told him.

'Huffing, he is, see,' said Bronwen, unnecessarily.

There was a crash of something thrown with force, and the sound of a neighbour's voice cursing. Hwyl reluctantly decided that he had better get up and investigate.

Everything in the yard looked as usual, except for the presence of a large tin-can which was clearly the object thrown. There was, however, a strong smell of burning, and a thudding noise, recognizable as the sound of the dragon tramping round and round in his hutch to stamp out the bedding caught alight again. Hwyl went across and opened the door. He raked out the smouldering straw, fetched some fresh, and threw it in.

'Quiet, you,' he told the dragon. 'More of this, and the hide I will have off you, slow and painful, too. Bed, now then, and sleep.'

He went back to bed himself, but it seemed as if he had only just laid his head on the pillow when it was daylight, and there was Idris Bowen hammering on the front door again.

Idris was more than a little incoherent, but Hwyl gathered that something further had taken place at his house, so he slipped on jacket and trousers, and went down. Idris led the way down beside his own house, and threw open the yard door with the air of a conjuror. Hwyl stared for some moments without speaking.

In front of Idris' henhouse stood a kind of trap, roughly contrived of angle-iron and wire-netting. In it, surrounded by chicken feathers, and glaring at them from eyes like live topazes, sat a creature, blood-red all over.

'Now, there is a dragon for you, indeed,' Idris said. 'Not to have colours like you see on a merry-go-round at a circus, either. A serious dragon, that one, and proper—wings, too, see?'

Hwyl went on looking at the dragon without a word. The wings were folded at present, and the cage did not give room to stretch them. The red, he saw now, was darker on the back, and brighter beneath, giving it the rather ominous effect of being lit from below by a blast-furnace. It certainly had a more practical aspect than his own dragon, and a fiercer look about it, altogether. He stepped forward to examine it more closely.

'Careful, man,' Idris warned him, laying a hand on his arm.

The dragon curled back its lips, and snorted. Twin flames a yard long shot out of its nostrils. It was a far better huff than the other dragon had ever achieved. The air was filled with a strong smell of burnt feathers.

'A fine dragon, that is,' Idris said again. 'A real Welsh dragon for you. Angry he is, see, and no wonder. A shocking thing for an imperialist dragon to be in his country. Come to throw him out, he has, and mincemeat he will be making of your namby-pamby, best-parlour dragon, too.'

'Better for him not to try,' said Hwyl, stouter in word than heart.

'And another thing, too. Red this dragon is, and so a real people's dragon, see.'

'Now then. Now then. Propaganda with dragons again, is it? Red the Welsh dragon has been two thousand years, and a fighter, too, I grant you. But a fighter for Wales, look; not just a loud-mouth talker of fighting for peace, see. If it is a good red Welsh dragon he is, then out of some kind of egg laid by your Uncle Joe, he is not; and thankful, too, I think,' Hwyl told him. 'And look you,' he added as an afterthought, 'this one it is who is stealing your chickens, not mine, at all.'

'Oh, let him have the old chickens, and glad,' Idris said. 'Here he is come to chase a foreign imperialist dragon out of his rightful territory, and a proper thing it is, too. None of your DP dragons are we wanting round Llynllawn, or South Wales, either.'

'Get you to hell, man,' Hwyl told him. 'Sweet dispositioned my dragon is, no bother to anyone, and no robber of henhouses, either. If there is trouble at all, the law I will be having of you and your dragon for disturbing of the peace, see. So I am telling you. And goodbye, now.'

He exchanged another glance with the angry-looking, topaz eyes of the red dragon, and then stalked away, back to his own house.

That evening, just as Hwyl was sitting down to his meal, there was a knock at the front door. Bronwen went to answer it, and came back.

'Ivor Thomas and Dafydd Ellis wanting you. Something about the Union,' she told him.

He went to see them. They had a long and involved story about dues that seemed not to have been fully paid. Hwyl was certain that he was paid-up to date, but they remained unconvinced. The argument went on for some time before, with head-shaking and reluctance, they consented to leave. Hwyl returned to the kitchen. Bronwen was waiting, standing by the table.

'Taken the dragon off, they have,' she said, flatly.

Hwyl stared at her. The reason why he had been kept at the front door in pointless argument suddenly came to him. He crossed to the window, and looked out. The back fence had been pushed flat, and a crowd of men carrying the dragon's hutch on their shoulders was already a hundred yards beyond it. Turning round, he saw Bronwen standing resolutely against the back door.

'Stealing, it is, and you not calling,' he said accusingly.

'Knocked you down, they would, and got the dragon just the same,' she said. 'Idris Bowen and his lot, it is.'

Hwyl looked out of the window again.

'What to do with him, now then?' he asked.

'Dragon fight, it is,' she told him. 'Betting, they

were. Five to one on the Welsh dragon, and sounding very sure, too.'

Hwyl shook his head.

'Not to wonder, either. There is not fair, at all. Wings, that Welsh dragon has, so air attacks he can make. Unsporting, there is, and shameful indeed.'

He looked out of the window again. More men were joining the party as it marched its burden across the waste-ground, towards the slag-heap. He sighed.

'There is sorry I am for our dragon. Murder it will be, I think. But go and see it, I will. So no tricks from that Idris to make a dirty fight dirtier.'

Bronwen hesitated.

'No fighting for you? You promise me?' she said.

'Is it a fool I am, girl, to be fighting fifty men, and more. Please to grant me some brains, now.'

She moved doubtfully out of his way, and let him open the door. Then she snatched up a scarf, and ran after him, tying it over her head as she went.

The crowd that was gathering on a piece of flat ground near the foot of the slag-heap already consisted of something more like a hundred men than fifty, and there were more hurrying to join it. Several self-constituted stewards were herding people back to clear an oval space. At one end of it was the cage in which the red dragon crouched huddled, with a bad-tempered look. At the other, the asbestos hutch was set down, and its bearers withdrew. Idris noticed Hwyl and Bronwen as they came up.

'And how much is it you are putting on your dragon?' he inquired, with a grin.

Bronwen said, before Hwyl could reply:

'Wicked, it is, and shamed you should be, Idris Bowen. Clip your dragon's wings to fight fair, and we will see. But betting against a horseshoe in the glove, we are not.' And she dragged Hwyl away.

All about the oval the laying of bets went on, with the Welsh dragon gaining favour all the time. Presently, Idris stepped out into the open, and held up his hands for quiet.

'Sport it is for you tonight. Super colossal attractions, as they are saying on the movies, and never again, likely. So put you your money, now. When the English law is hearing of this, no more dragon-fighting, it will be—like no more to cockfight.' A boo went up, mingled with the laughter of those who knew a thing or two about cockfighting that the English law did not. Idris went on: 'So now the dragon championship, I am giving you. On my sight, the Red Dragon of Wales, on his home ground. A people's dragon, see. For more than a coincidence, it is, that the colour of the Welsh dragon—' His voice was lost for some moments in controversial shouts. It re-emerged, saying: '—left, the decadent dragon of the imperialist exploiters of the suffering Chinese people who, in their glorious fight for peace under the heroic leadership—' But the rest of his introduction was also lost among the catcalls and cheers that were still continuing when he beckoned forward attendants from the ends of the oval, and withdrew.

At one end, two men reached up with a hooked pole, pulled over the contraption that enclosed the red dragon, and ran back hurriedly. At the far end, a man knocked the peg from the asbestos door, pulled it open, scuttled round behind the hutch, and no less speedily out of harm's way.

The red dragon looked round, uncertainly. It tentatively tried unfurling its wings. Finding that possible, it reared up on its hind legs, supporting itself on its tail, and flapped them energetically, as though to dispel the creases.

The other dragon ambled out of its hutch, advanced a few feet, and stood blinking. Against the background of the waste-ground and the slag-heap it looked more than usually exotic. It yawned largely, with a fine display of fangs, rolled its eyes hither and thither, and then caught sight of the red dragon.

Simultaneously, the red dragon noticed the other. It stopped flapping, and dropped to all four feet. The two regarded one another. A hush came over the crowd. Both dragons remained motionless, except for a slight waving of the last foot or so of their tails.

The oriental dragon turned its head a little on one side. It snorted slightly, and shrivelled up a patch of weeds.

The red dragon stiffened. It suddenly adopted a pose gardant, one forefoot uplifted with claws extended, wings raised. It huffed with vigour, vapourized a puddle, and disappeared momentarily in a cloud of steam. There was an anticipatory murmur from the crowd.

The red dragon began to pace round, circling the other, giving a slight flap of its wings now and then.

The crowd watched it intently. So did the other dragon. It did not move from its position, but turned as the red dragon circled, keeping its head and gaze steadily towards it.

With the circle almost completed, the red dragon halted. It extended its wings widely, and gave a full-throated roar. Simultaneously, it gushed two streams of fire, and belched a small cloud of black smoke. The part of the crowd nearest to it moved back, apprehensively.

At this tense moment Bronwen Hughes began suddenly to laugh. Hwyl shook her by the arm.

'Hush, you! There is not funny, at all,' he said, but she did not stop at once.

The oriental dragon did nothing for a moment. It appeared to be thinking the matter over. Then it turned swiftly round, and began to run. The crowd behind it raised a jeer, those in front waved their arms to shoo it back. But the dragon was unimpressed by arm-waving. It came on, with now and then a short spurt of flame from its nostrils. The people wavered, and then scattered out of its way. Half a dozen men started to chase after it with sticks, but soon gave up. It was travelling at twice the pace they could run.

With a roar, the red dragon leapt into the air, and came across the field, spitting flames like a strafing aircraft. The crowd scattered still more swiftly, tumbling over itself as it cleared a way.

The running dragon disappeared round the foot of the slag-heap, with the other hovering above it. Shouts of disappointment rose from the crowd, and a good part of it started to follow, to be in at the death.

But in a minute or two the running dragon came into view again. It was making a fine pace up the mountainside, with the red dragon still flying a little behind it. Everybody stood watching it wind its way up and up until, finally, it disappeared over the shoulder. For a moment the flying dragon still showed as a black silhouette above the skyline, then, with a final whiff of flame, it, too, disappeared—and the arguments about paying up began.

Idris left the wrangling to come across to the Hugheses.

'So there is a coward your imperialist dragon is, then. And not one good huff, or a bite to him, either,' he said.

Bronwen looked at him, and smiled.

'So foolish, you are, Idris Bowen, with your head full of propaganda and fighting. Other things than to fight, there is, even for dragons. Such a brave show your red dragon was making, such a fine show, oh, yes—and very like a peacock, I am thinking. Very like the boys in their Sunday suits in Llangolwgcoch High Street, too—all dressed up to kill, but not to fight.'

Idris stared at her.

'And our dragon,' she went on. 'Well, there is not a very new trick, either. Done a bit of it before now, I have, myself.' She cast a sidelong glance at Hwyl.

Light began to dawn on Idris.

'But—but it is *he* you were always calling your dragon,' he protested.

Bronwen shrugged.

'Oh, yes, indeed. But how to tell with dragons?' she asked.

She turned to look up the mountain.

'There is lonely, lonely the red dragon must have

been these two thousand years—so not much bothering with your politics, he is, just now. More single
with his mind, see. And interesting it will be, indeed,
to be having a lot of baby dragons in Wales before
long, I am thinking.'

*   *   *

JOHN WYNDHAM learned all about dragons from
his Welsh parents and many of his later fantasy stories
reveal his interest in the folk lore and traditions of
that country. His early tales, though, were mainly
science fiction stories about distant plants such as
Mars and Venus for American magazines. But in 1951
he published a frightening novel of an alien invasion
of the Earth, *The Day of the Triffids*, which became a
best-seller and was later filmed. Further groundbreaking novels helped to secure his fame including
The Kraken Wakes (1953) about a terrifying sea monster and *Village of the Damned* (1960) in which the
offspring of aliens gradually take over a small English
village. Throughout the 1960s, John Wyndham
was one of the best read sf authors and for years his
most famous books appeared regularly on school
syllabuses.

THE WISH

Roald Dahl

Transfiguration is another of the wizard's great tricks. By the use of magic they can completely change the structure and appearance of something. A frog can become a man, a stone may turn into a bird, and an iron rod change into a snake. Wizards also have the power to turn patterns and pictures into living tableaux. A famous example of this ability to metamorphose things by the power of the will can found in T. H. White's book, The Sword and the Stone, *in which Merlin transforms his young pupil, Arthur, into various animals. In the last story we read all about dragons and in this next one it is the turn of snakes—transfigured snakes brought alive by mind-power. The little boy in the tale is fascinated by snakes of all shapes, sizes and colours and they ultimately lead him into a dangerous game. He doesn't have a name—he could be James or Charlie or even Harry—but like any boy (and many girls, for that matter) he's curious about magic. The secret things suggested by everyday objects and also mystic squares and deep, dark holes that may just be the entrance-ways to strange worlds. So do tread carefully with him into the next few pages— and be sure not to suffer the same fate . . .*

*   *   *

Under the palm of one hand the child became aware of the scab of an old cut on his kneecap. He bent forward to examine it closely. A scab was always a fascinating thing; it presented a special challenge he was never able to resist.

Yes, he thought, I will pick it off, even if it isn't ready, even if the middle of it sticks, even if it hurts like anything.

With a fingernail he began to explore cautiously around the edges of the scab. He got the nail underneath it, and when he raised it, but ever so slightly, it suddenly came off, the whole hard brown scab came off beautifully, leaving an interesting little circle of smooth red skin.

Nice. Very nice indeed. He rubbed the circle and it didn't hurt. He picked up the scab, put it on his thigh and flipped it with a finger so that it flew away and landed on the edge of the carpet, the enormous red and black and yellow carpet that stretched the whole length of the hall from the stairs on which he sat to the front door in the distance. A tremendous carpet. Bigger than the tennis lawn. Much bigger than that. He regarded it gravely, settling his eyes upon it with mild pleasure. He had never really noticed it before, but now, all of a sudden, the colours seemed to brighten mysteriously and spring out at him in a most dazzling way.

You see, he told himself, I know how it is. The red parts of the carpet are red-hot lumps of coal. What I must do is this: I must walk all the way along it to the front door without touching them. If I touch the red I will be burnt. As a matter of fact, I will be burnt up completely. And the black parts of the carpet . . .

yes, the black parts are snakes, poisonous snakes, adders mostly, and cobras, thick like tree-trunks round the middle, and if I touch one of *them*, I'll be bitten and I'll die before tea time. And if I get across safely, without being burnt and without being bitten, I will be given a puppy for my birthday tomorrow.

He got to his feet and climbed higher up the stairs to obtain a better view of this vast tapestry of colour and death. Was it possible? Was there enough yellow? Yellow was the only colour he was allowed to walk on. Could it be done? This was not a journey to be undertaken lightly; the risks were too great for that. The child's face—a fringe of white-gold hair, two large blue eyes, a small pointed chin—peered down anxiously over the banisters. The yellow was a bit thin in places and there were one or two widish gaps, but it did seem to go all the way along to the other end. For someone who had only yesterday triumphantly travelled the whole length of the brick path from the stables to the summer-house without touching the cracks, this carpet thing should not be too difficult. Except for the snakes. The mere thought of snakes sent a fine electricity of fear running like pins down the backs of his legs and under the soles of his feet.

He came slowly down the stairs and advanced to the edge of the carpet. He extended one small sandalled foot and placed it cautiously upon a patch of yellow. Then he brought the other foot up, and there was just enough room for him to stand with the two feet together. There! He had started! His bright oval face was curiously intent, a shade whiter perhaps than before, and he was holding his arms out sideways to assist his balance. He took another step, lifting his foot high over a patch of black, aiming carefully with his toe for a narrow channel of yellow on the other side. When he had completed the second step he paused to rest, standing very stiff and still. The narrow channel of yellow ran forward unbroken for at least five yards and he advanced gingerly along it, bit by bit, as though walking a tightrope. Where it finally curled off sideways, he had to take another long stride, this time over a vicious-looking mixture of black and red. Halfway across he began to wobble. He waved his arms around wildly, windmill fashion, to keep his balance, and he got across safely and rested again on the other side. He was quite breathless now, and so tense he stood high on his toes all the time, arms out sideways, fists clenched. He was on a big safe island of yellow. There was lots of room on it, he couldn't possibly fall off, and he stood there resting, hesitating, waiting, wishing he could stay for ever on this big safe yellow island. But the fear of not getting the puppy compelled him to go on.

Step by step, he edged further ahead, and between each one he paused to decide exactly where next he should put his foot. Once, he had a choice of ways, either to left or right, and he chose the left because although it seemed the more difficult, there was not so much black in that direction. The black was what made him nervous. He glanced quickly over his shoulder to see how far he had come. Nearly halfway. There could be no turning back now. He was in the middle and he couldn't turn back and he couldn't jump off sideways either because it was too far, and when he looked at all the red and all the black that lay ahead of him, he felt that old sudden sickening surge of panic in his chest—like last Easter time, that afternoon when he got lost all alone in the darkest part of Piper's Wood.

He took another step, placing his foot carefully upon the only little piece of yellow within reach, and this time the point of the foot came within a centimetre of some black. It wasn't touching the black, he could see it wasn't touching, he could see the small line of yellow separating the toe of his sandal from the black; but the snake stirred as though sensing the nearness, and raised its head and gazed at the foot with bright beady eyes, watching to see if it was going to touch.

'*I'm not touching you! You mustn't bite me! You know I'm not touching you!*'

Another snake slid up noiselessly beside the first, raised its head, two heads now, two pairs of eyes staring at the foot, gazing at a little naked place just below the sandal strap where the skin showed through. The child went high up on his toes and stayed there, frozen stiff with terror. It was minutes before he dared to move again.

The next step would have to be a really long one. There was this deep curling river of black that ran clear across the width of the carpet, and he was forced by this position to cross it at its widest part. He thought first of trying to jump it, but decided he couldn't be sure of landing accurately on the narrow band of yellow the other side. He took a deep breath, lifted one foot, and inch by inch he pushed it out in front of him, far far out, then down and down until at last the tip of his sandal was across and resting safely on the edge of the yellow. He leaned forward, transferring his weight to his front foot. Then he tried to bring the back foot up as well. He strained and pulled and jerked his body, but the legs were too wide apart and he couldn't make it. He tried to get back again. He couldn't do that either. He was doing the splits and he was properly stuck. He glanced down and saw this deep curling river of black underneath him. Parts of it were stirring now, and uncoiling and sliding and beginning to shine with a dreadfully oily glister. He wobbled, waved his arms frantically to keep his balance, but that seemed to make it worse. He was starting to go over. He was going over to the right, quite slowly he was going over, then faster and faster, and at the last moment, instinctively he put out a hand to break the fall and the next thing he saw was this bare hand of his going right into the middle of a great glistening mass of black and he gave one piercing cry of terror as it touched.

Outside in the sunshine, far away behind the house, the mother was looking for her son.

*   *   *

ROALD DAHL is one of the biggest-selling authors of children's stories in the world. Yet, as he admitted, he didn't like school much, was a bit of a nuisance and was disliked by his teachers because he was so unpredictable. Indeed, one of his English teachers wrote, 'I have never met anybody who so persistently writes words meaning the exact opposite of what is intended'. During the Second World War, Dahl was a pilot in the RAF and had a terrible crash which fractured his skull. But, as he said later, 'You do get bits of magic from enormous bumps on the head', and he turned his vivid imagination into writing fantasies for younger readers like *James and the Giant Peach* (1961), *The Magic Finger* (1966) and *The Witches* (1983). The success of these books resulted in the foundation of the Roald Dahl Children's Gallery in Aylesbury not far from where he lived. Visitors can discover everything they need to know about magic-makers in Matilda's library, as well as having lots of bogsquiffling entertainment and buzzwangling fun. The illusions in the gallery are as good as those described in this story—but everyone who goes there should always remember Roald Dahl's warning: 'Those who don't believe in magic will never find it.'

INVISIBLE BOY

Ray Bradbury

Who wouldn't like the power to become invisible? Wizards claim to have found the secret centuries ago, and Charlie, the hero of this next story, also wants the power to be able to walk about so that no one can see him. He's a resourceful kid whose parents abandoned him so he's run off to live with his aunt who lives in an isolated old cabin. She just happens to be a witch. The old lady does know a lot about magic, though, and she uses all sorts of strange ingredients in her spells such as mummified frog and raw bat. She also likes Charlie a lot and wants to teach him the secrets of her art. Things like how to make animals stop in their tracks; how to unbewitch a goat; and even how to become bullet-proof. The trouble is, the old lady's magic does not always *work . . .*

*　　　*　　　*

She took the great iron spoon and the mummified frog and gave it a bash and made dust of it, and talked to the dust while she ground it in her stony fists quickly. Her beady gray bird-eyes flickered at the cabin. Each time she looked, a head in the small thin window ducked as if she'd fired off a shotgun.

'Charlie!' cried Old Lady. 'You come outa there! I'm fixing a lizard magic to unlock that rusty door!'

You come out now and I won't make the earth shake or the trees go up in fire or the sun set at high noon!'

The only sound was the warm mountain light on the high turpentine trees, a tufted squirrel chittering around and around on a green-furred log, the ants moving in a fine brown line at Old Lady's bare, blue-veined feet.

'You been starving in there two days, darn you!' she panted, chiming the spoon against a flat rock, causing the plump gray miracle bag to swing at her waist. Sweating sour, she rose and marched at the cabin, bearing the pulverized flesh. 'Come out, now!' She flicked a pinch of powder inside the lock. 'All right, I'll come get you!' she wheezed.

She spun the knob with one walnut-colored hand, first one way, then the other. 'O Lord,' she intoned, 'fling this door wide!'

When nothing flung, she added yet another philter and held her breath. Her long blue untidy skirt rustled as she peered into her bag of darkness to see if she had any scaly monsters there, any charm finer than the frog she'd killed months ago for such a crisis as this.

She heard Charlie breathing against the door. His folks had pranced off into some Ozark town early this week, leaving him, and he'd run almost six miles to Old Lady for company—she was by way of being an aunt or cousin or some such, and he didn't mind her fashions.

But then, two days ago, Old Lady, having gotten used to the boy around, decided to keep him for convenient company. She pricked her thin shoulder bone, drew out three blood pearls, spat wet over her right elbow, tromped on a crunch-cricket, and at the same instant clawed her left hand at Charlie, crying, 'My son you are, you are my son, for all eternity!'

Charlie, bounding like a startled hare, had crashed off into the bush, heading for home.

But Old Lady, skittering quick as a gingham lizard, cornered him in a dead end, and Charlie holed up in this old hermit's cabin and wouldn't come out, no matter how she whammed door, window, or knothole with amber-colored fist or trounced her ritual fires, explaining to him that he was certainly her son *now*, all right.

'Charlie, *you there?*' she asked, cutting holes in the door planks with her bright little slippery eyes.

'I'm all of me here,' he replied finally, very tired.

Maybe he would fall out on the ground any moment. She wrestled the knob hopefully. Perhaps a pinch too much frog powder had grated the lock wrong. She always overdid or underdid her miracles, she mused angrily, never doing them just *exact*, Devil take it!

'Charlie, I only wants someone to night-prattle to, someone to warm hands with at the fire. Someone to fetch kindling for me mornings, and fight off the spunks that come creeping of early fogs! I ain't got no fetchings on you for myself, son, just for your company.' She smacked her lips. 'Tell you what, Charles, you come out and I *teach* you things!'

'What things?' he suspicioned.

'Teach you how to buy cheap, sell high. Catch a snow weasel, cut off its head, carry it warm in your hind pocket. There!'

'Aw,' said Charlie.

She made haste. 'Teach you to make yourself shot-proof. So if anyone bangs at you with a gun, nothing happens.'

When Charlie stayed silent, she gave him the secret in a high fluttering whisper. 'Dig and stitch mouse-ear roots on Friday during full moon, and wear 'em around your neck in a white silk.'

'You're *crazy*,' Charlie said.

'Teach you how to stop blood or make animals stand frozen or make blind horses see, all them things I'll teach you! Teach you to cure a swelled-up cow and unbewitch a goat. Show you how to make yourself invisible!'

'Oh,' said Charlie.

Old Lady's heart beat like a Salvation tambourine.

The knob turned from the other side.

'You,' said Charlie, 'are funning me.'

'No, I'm not,' exclaimed Old Lady. 'Oh, Charlie, why, I'll make you like a window, see right through you. Why, child, you'll be surprised!'

'Real invisible?'

'Real invisible!'

'You won't fetch onto me if I walk out?'

'Won't touch a bristle of you, son.'

'Well,' he drawled reluctantly, 'all right.'

The door opened. Charlie stood in his bare feet, head down, chin against chest. 'Make me invisible,' he said.

'First we got to catch us a bat,' said Old Lady. 'Start lookin'!'

She gave him some jerky beef for his hunger and watched him climb a tree. He went high up and high up and it was nice seeing him there and it was nice having him here and all about after so many years alone with nothing to say good morning to but bird-droppings and silvery snail tracks.

Pretty soon a bat with a broken wing fluttered down out of the tree. Old Lady snatched it up, beating warm and shrieking between its porcelain white teeth, and Charlie dropped down after it, hand upon clenched hand, yelling.

That night, with the moon nibbling at the spiced pine cones, Old Lady extracted a long silver needle from under her wide blue dress. Gumming her excitement and secret anticipation, she sighted up the dead bat and held the cold needle steady-steady.

She had long ago realized that her miracles, despite all perspirations and salts and sulphurs, failed. But she had always dreamt that one day the miracles might start functioning, might spring up in crimson flowers and silver stars to prove that God had forgiven her for her pink body and her pink thoughts and her warm body and her warm thoughts as a young miss. But so far God had made no sign and said no word, but nobody knew this except Old Lady.

'Ready?' she asked Charlie, who crouched cross-kneed, wrapping his pretty legs in long goose-pimpled arms, his mouth open, making teeth. 'Ready,' he whispered, shivering.

'There!' She plunged the needle deep in the bat's right eye. 'So!'

'Oh!' screamed Charlie, wadding up his face.

'Now I wrap it in gingham, and here, put it in your pocket, keep it there, bat and all. Go on!'

He pocketed the charm.

'Charlie!' she shrieked fearfully. 'Charlie, where *are* you? I can't *see* you, child!'

'Here!' He jumped so the light ran in red streaks up his body. 'I'm here, Old Lady!' He stared wildly at his arms, legs, chest, and toes. 'I'm here!'

Her eyes looked as if they were watching a thousand fireflies crisscrossing each other in the wild night air.

'Charlie, oh, you went *fast*! Quick as a hummingbird! Oh, Charlie, come *back* to me!'

'But I'm *here*!' he wailed.

'Where?'

'By the fire, the fire! And—and I can see myself. I'm not invisible at all!'

Old Lady rocked on her lean flanks. 'Course *you* can see *you*! Every invisible person knows himself. Otherwise, how could you eat, walk, or get around places? Charlie, touch me. Touch me so I *know* you.'

Uneasily he put out a hand.

She pretended to jerk, startled, at his touch. '*Ah!*'

'You mean to say you can't *find* me?' he asked. 'Truly?'

'Not the least half-rump of you!'

She found a tree to stare at, and stared at it with shining eyes, careful not to glance at him. 'Why, I sure *did* a trick *that* time!' She sighed with wonder. 'Whooeee. Quickest invisible I *ever* made! Charlie. Charlie, how you *feel*?'

'Like creek water—all stirred.'

'You'll settle.'

Then after a pause she added, 'Well, what you going to do now, Charlie, since you're invisible?'

All sorts of things shot through his brain, she could

tell. Adventures stood up and danced like hell-fire in his eyes, and his mouth, just hanging, told what it meant to be a boy who imagined himself like the mountain winds. In a cold dream he said, 'I'll run across wheat fields, climb snow mountains, steal white chickens off'n farms. I'll kick pink pigs when they ain't looking. I'll pinch pretty girls' legs when they sleep, snap their garters in schoolrooms.' Charlie looked at Old Lady, and from the shiny tips of her eyes she saw something wicked shape his face. 'And other things I'll do, I'll do, I will,' he said.

'Don't try nothing on me,' warned Old Lady. 'I'm brittle as spring ice and I don't take handling.' Then: 'What about your folks?'

'My folks?'

'You can't fetch yourself home looking like that. Scare the inside ribbons out of them. Your mother'd faint straight back like timber falling. Think they want you about the house to stumble over and your ma have to call you every three minutes, even though you're in the room next her elbow?'

Charlie had not considered it. He sort of simmered down and whispered out a little 'Gosh' and felt of his long bones carefully.

'You'll be mighty lonesome. People looking through you like a water glass, people knocking you aside because they didn't reckon you to be underfoot. And women, Charlie, *women*—'

He swallowed. 'What about women?'

'No woman will be giving you a second stare. And no woman wants to be kissed by a boy's mouth they can't even *find*!'

Charlie dug his bare toe in the soil contemplatively.

He pouted. 'Well, I'll stay invisible, anyway, for a spell. I'll have me some fun. I'll just be pretty careful, is all. I'll stay out from in front of wagons and horses and Pa. Pa shoots at the nariest sound.' Charlie blinked. 'Why, with me invisible, someday Pa might just up and fill me with buckshot, thinkin' I was a hill squirrel in the dooryard. Oh . . .'

Old Lady nodded at a tree. 'That's likely.'

'Well,' he decided slowly, 'I'll stay invisible for tonight, and tomorrow you can fix me back all whole again, Old Lady.'

'Now if that ain't just like a critter, always wanting to be what he can't be,' remarked Old Lady to a beetle on a log.

'What you mean?' said Charlie.

'Why,' she explained, 'it was real hard work, fixing you up. It'll take a little *time* for it to wear off. Like a coat of paint wears off, boy.'

'You!' he cried. 'You did this to me! Now you make me back, you make me seeable!'

'Hush,' she said. 'It'll wear off, a hand or a foot at a time.'

'How'll it look, me around the hills with just one hand showing!'

'Like a five-winged bird hopping on the stones and bramble.'

'Or a foot showing!'

'Like a small pink rabbit jumping thicket.'

'Or my head floating!'

'Like a hairy balloon at the carnival!'

'How long before I'm *whole*?' he asked.

She deliberated that it might pretty well be an entire year.

He groaned. He began to sob and bite his lips and make fists. 'You magicked me, you did this, you did this thing to me. Now I won't be able to run home!'

She winked. 'But you *can* stay here, child, stay on with me real comfort-like, and I'll keep you fat and saucy.'

He flung it out: 'You did this on purpose! You mean old hag, you want to keep me here!'

He ran off through the shrubs on the instant.

'Charlie, come back!'

No answer but the pattern of his feet on the soft dark turf, and his wet choking cry which passed swiftly off and away.

She waited and then kindled herself a fire. 'He'll be back,' she whispered. And thinking inward on herself, she said, 'And now I'll have me my company through spring and into late summer. Then, when I'm tired of him and want a silence, I'll send him home.'

Charlie returned noiselessly with the first gray of dawn, gliding over the rimed turf to where Old Lady sprawled like a bleached stick before the scattered ashes.

He sat on some creek pebbles and stared at her.

She didn't dare look at him or beyond. He had made no sound, so how could she know he was anywhere about? She couldn't.

He sat there, tear marks on his cheeks.

Pretending to be just waking—but she had found no sleep from one end of the night to the other—Old Lady stood up, grunting and yawning, and turned in a circle to the dawn.

'Charlie?'

Her eyes passed from pines to soil, to sky, to the far hills. She called out his name, over and over again, and she felt like staring plumb straight at him, but she stopped herself. 'Charlie? Oh, Charles!' she called, and heard the echoes say the very same.

He sat, beginning to grin a bit, suddenly, knowing he was close to her, yet she must feel alone. Perhaps he felt the growing of a secret power, perhaps he felt secure from the world, certainly he was *pleased* with his invisibility.

She said aloud, 'Now where *can* that boy be? If he only made a noise so I could tell just where he is, maybe I'd fry him a breakfast.'

She prepared the morning victuals, irritated at his continuous quiet. She sizzled bacon on a hickory stick. 'The smell of it will draw his nose,' she muttered.

While her back was turned he swiped all the frying bacon and devoured it tastily.

She whirled, crying out, 'Lord!'

She eyed the clearing suspiciously. 'Charlie, that *you?*'

Charlie wiped his mouth clean on his wrists.

She trotted about the clearing, making like she was trying to locate him. Finally, with a clever thought, acting blind, she headed straight for him, groping. 'Charlie, where *are* you?'

A lightning streak, he evaded her, bobbing, ducking.

It took all her will power not to give chase; but you can't chase invisible boys, so she sat down, scowling, sputtering, and tried to fry more bacon. But every fresh strip she cut he would steal bubbling off the fire and run away far. Finally, cheeks burning, she cried, 'I know where you are! Right *there*! I hear you run!' She pointed to one side of him, not too accurate. He ran again. 'Now you're there!' she shouted. 'There, and there!' pointing to all the places he was in the next five minutes. 'I hear you press a grass blade, knock a flower, snap a twig. I got fine shell ears, delicate as roses. They can hear the stars moving!'

Silently he galloped off among the pines, his voice trailing back, 'Can't hear me when I'm set on a rock. I'll just *set*!'

All day he sat on an observatory rock in the clear wind, motionless and sucking his tongue.

Old Lady gathered wood in the deep forest, feeling his eyes weaseling on her spine. She wanted to babble: 'Oh, I see you, I see you! I was only fooling about invisible boys! You're right there!' But she swallowed her gall and gummed it tight.

The following morning he did the spiteful things. He began leaping from behind trees. He made toad-faces, frog-faces, spider-faces at her, clenching down his lips with his fingers, popping his raw eyes, pushing up his nostrils so you could peer in and see his brain thinking.

Once she dropped her kindling. She pretended it was a blue jay startled her.

He made a motion as if to strangle her.

She trembled a little.

He made another move as if to bang her shins and spit on her cheek.

These motions she bore without a lid-flicker or a mouth-twitch.

He stuck out his tongue, making strange bad noises. He wiggled his loose ears so she wanted to laugh, and finally she did laugh and explained it away quickly by saying, 'Sat on a salamander! Whew, how it poked!'

By high noon the whole madness boiled to a terrible peak.

For it was at that exact hour that Charlie came racing down the valley stark boy-naked!

Old Lady nearly fell flat with shock!

'Charlie!' she almost cried.

Charlie raced naked up one side of a hill and naked down the other—naked as day, naked as the moon, raw as the sun and a newborn chick, his feet shimmering and rushing like the wings of a low-skimming hummingbird.

Old Lady's tongue locked in her mouth. What could she say? Charlie, go dress? For *shame*? *Stop* that? *Could* she? Oh, Charlie, Charlie, God! Could she say that now? *Well*?

Upon the big rock, she witnessed him dancing up and down, naked as the day of his birth, stomping bare feet, smacking his hands on his knees and sucking in and out his white stomach like blowing and deflating a circus balloon.

She shut her eyes tight and prayed.

After three hours of this she pleaded, 'Charlie, Charlie, come here! I got something to *tell* you!'

Like a fallen leaf he came, dressed again, praise the Lord.

'Charlie,' she said, looking at the pine trees, 'I see your right toe. *There* it is.'

'You do?' he said.

'Yes,' she said very sadly. 'There it is like a horny toad on the grass. And there, up there's your left ear hanging on the air like a pink butterfly.'

Charlie danced. 'I'm forming in, I'm forming in!'

Old Lady nodded. 'Here comes your ankle!'

'Gimme *both* my feet!' ordered Charlie.

'You got 'em.'

'How about my hands?'

'I see one crawling on your knee like a daddy longlegs.'

'How about the other one?'

'It's crawling too.'

'I got a body?'

'Shaping up fine.'

'I'll need my head to go home, Old Lady.'

To go home, she thought wearily. 'No!' she said, stubborn and angry. 'No, you ain't got no head. No head at all,' she cried. She'd leave that to the very last. 'No head, no head,' she insisted.

'No head?' he wailed.

'Yes, oh my God, yes, yes, you got your blamed head!' she snapped, giving up. 'Now, fetch me back my bat with the needle in his eye!'

He flung it at her. 'Haaaa-yoooo!' His yelling went all up the valley, and long after he had run toward home she heard his echoes, racing.

Then she plucked up her kindling with a great dry weariness and started back toward her shack, sighing, talking. And Charlie followed her all the way, *really* invisible now, so she couldn't see him, just hear him, like a pine cone dropping or a deep underground stream trickling, or a squirrel clambering a bough; and over the fire at twilight she and Charlie sat, him so invisible, and her feeding him bacon he wouldn't take, so she ate it herself, and then she fixed some magic and fell asleep with Charlie, made out of sticks and rags and pebbles, but still warm and her very own son, slumbering and nice in her shaking mother arms . . . and they talked about golden things in drowsy voices until dawn made the fire slowly, slowly wither out. . . .

*   *   *

RAY BRADBURY has written some of the most imaginative fantasy stories about childhood, a lot of them based on his own rural upbringing in the Midwest of America. Although he was taken with his family to Los Angeles in 1934, he never forget the joys of growing up and the central character in many of his short stories is a boy called Douglas who is very much himself. One of Bradbury's first major creations was a series of stories about a family consisting of a group of supernatural beings who all live together in an everyday home. His reputation was established with *Dandelion Wine* (1950) which brought together many of the Douglas stories, followed by a terrifying novel of the future, *Fahrenheit 451* (1953), predicting a time when all books will be burned to prevent ideas being circulated, and a supernatural thriller, *Something Wicked This Way Comes* (1962), in which two teenage boys become trapped in the side-shows of a travelling carnival. Ray Bradbury's fascination with magic can also be seen in a number of his other short stories including 'Fever Dream,' 'The Traveller' and 'The Burning Man' plus his fine juvenile novel, *The Hallowe'en Tree* (1972).

MY NAME IS DOLLY

William F. Nolan

Although wizards, by and large, do not use their magic to harm people, they have always been quick to take action on behalf of ill-treated children. Some, perhaps, have memories of their own childhood and the rigours they went through to become magicians. Adopted and single-parent children in particular have suffered at the hands of new adults entering their lives. Take Harry Potter, for example, being brought up by his Uncle Vernon and Aunt Petunia who have given him a hard time ever since the death of his mum and dad. Uncle Vernon is a pretty repulsive character, but perhaps not as genuinely nasty as Mr Brubaker in this next story. He literally terrifies the orphan Dorothy. Red-haired and freckle-faced, Dolly—as she is known to her friends— was adopted by the Brubakers and for a time, while Mrs Brubaker was alive, things were fine. But after Mrs Brubaker's sudden death, the old man has started to treat her in really unpleasant ways. So Dorothy goes to see Old Meg, a witch who lives in a boat-house, in the hope that she can put a spell on evil Mr Brubaker. To her surprise, what she is given to help her is a doll the very spitting image of herself...

*   *   *

Monday—Today I met the witch—which is a good place to start this diary. (I had to look up how to spell it. First I spelled it dairy but that's a place you get milk and from this you're going to get blood so it is plenty different.)

Let me tell you about Meg. She's maybe a thousand years old (A witch can live forever, right?) She's all gnarly like the bark of an oak tree, her skin I mean, and she has real big eyes. Like looking into deep dark caves and you don't know what's down there. Her nose is hooked and she has sharp teeth like a cat's are. When she smiles some of them are missing. Her hair is all wild and clumpy and she smells bad. Guess she hasn't had a shower for a real long time. Wears a long black dress with holes bit in it. By rats most likely. She lives in this old deserted cobwebby boathouse they don't use anymore on the lake—and it's full of fat gray rats. Old Meg doesn't seem to mind.

My name is Dolly. Short for Dorothy like in the Oz books. Only nobody ever calls me Dorothy. I'm still a kid and not very tall and I've got red hair and freckles. (I really *hate* freckles! When I was real little I tried to rub them off but you can't. They stick just like tattoos do.)

Reason I went out to the lake to see old Meg is because of how much I hate my father. Well, he's not really my father, since I'm adopted and I don't know my real father. Maybe he's a nice man and not like Mister Brubaker who adopted me. Mrs Brubaker died of the flu last winter which is when Mister Brubaker began to molest me. (I looked up the word molest and it's the right one for what he keeps trying to do with me.) When I won't let him he gets really mad and slaps me and I run out of the house until he's all calmed down again. Then he'll get special nice and offer me cookies with chocolate chunks in them which are my very favorite kind. He wants me to like him so he can molest me later.

Last week I heard about the witch who lives by the lake. A friend at school told me. Some of the kids used to go down there to throw rocks at her until she put a spell on Lucy Akins and Lucy ran away and no one's seen her since. Probably she's dead. The kids leave old Meg alone now.

I thought maybe Meg could put a spell on Mister Brubaker for five dollars. (I saved up that much.) Which is why I went to see her. She said she couldn't because she can't put spells on people unless she can see them up close and look in their eyes like she did to Lucy Akins.

The lake was black and smelly with big gas bubbles breaking in it and the boathouse was cold and damp and the nats scared me but old Meg was the only way I knew to get even with Mister Brubaker. She kept my five dollars and told me she was going into town soon and would look around for something to use against Mister Brubaker. I promised to come see her on Friday after school.

We'll have his blood, she said.

FRIDAY NIGHT—I went to see old Meg again and she gave me the doll to take home. A real big one, as tall as I am, with freckles and red hair just like mine. And in a pretty pink dress with little black slippers with red bows on them. The doll's eyes open and close and she has a big metal key in her back where you wind her up. When you do she opens her big dark eyes and says hello, my name is Dolly. Same as mine. I asked Meg where she found Dolly and she said at Mister Carter's toy store. But I've been in there lots of times and I've never seen a doll like this for five dollars. Take her home, Meg told me, and she'll be your friend. I was real excited and ran off pulling Dolly behind me. She has a box with wheels on it you put her inside and pull along the sidewalk.

She's too big to carry.

MONDAY—Mister Brubaker doesn't like Dolly. He says she's damn strange. That's his words, damn strange. But she's my new friend so I don't care what he says about her. He wouldn't let me take her to school.

SATURDAY—I took some of Mister Brubaker's hair to old Meg today. She asked me to cut some off while he was asleep at night and it was really hard to do without waking him up but I got some and gave it to her. She wanted me to bring Dolly and I did and Meg said that Dolly was going to be her agent. That's the word. Agent. (I try to get all the words right.)

Dolly had opened her deep dark eyes and seen Mister Brubaker and old Meg said that was all she needed. She wrapped two of Mister Brubaker's hairs around the big metal key in Dolly's back and told me not to wind her up again until Sunday afternoon when Mister Brubaker was home watching his sports. He always does that on Sunday.

So I said okay.

SUNDAY NIGHT—This afternoon, like always, Mister Brubaker was watching a sports game on the television when I set Dolly right in front of him and did just what old Meg told me to do. I wound her up with the big key and then took the key out of her back and put it in her right hand. It was long and sharp and Dolly opened her eyes and said hello, my name is Dolly and stuck the metal key in Mister Brubaker's chest. There was a lot of blood. (I told you there would be.)

Mister Brubaker picked Dolly up and threw the front of her into the fire. I mean, that's how she landed, just the front of her at the edge of the fire. (It's winter now, and real cold in the house without a fire.) After he did that he fell down and didn't get up. He was dead so I called Doctor Thompson.

The police came with him and rescued Dolly out of the fire when I told them what happened. Her nice red hair was mostly burnt away and the whole left side of her face was burnt real bad and the paint had all peeled back and blistered. And one of her arms had burnt clear off and her pink dress was all char-colored and with big fire holes in it. The policeman who rescued her said that a toy doll couldn't kill anybody and that I must have stuck the key into Mister Brubaker's chest and blamed it on Dolly. They took me away to a home for bad children.

I didn't tell anybody about old Meg.

TUESDAY—It is a long time later and my hair is real pretty now and my face is almost healed. The lady who runs this House says there will always be big scars on the left side of my face but I was lucky not to lose my eye on that side. It is hard to eat and play with the other kids with just one arm but that's okay because I can still hear Mister Brubaker screaming and see all the blood coming out of his chest and that's nice.

I wish I could tell old Meg thank you. I forgot to— and you should always thank people for doing nice things for you.

*   *   *

WILLIAM F. NOLAN is a great friend of the previous writer, Ray Bradbury, and the two men share an interest in the folk lore of childhood. A former commercial artist and racing car driver, Nolan is now well known for the novel, *Logan's Run* (1967), all about a future world where *everyone* on reaching the age of twenty-one is sentenced to be killed in order to prevent overpopulation. This chilling plot in which a young man and woman rebel against the death-threat and go on the run to avoid their fate, has since been filmed, inspired a TV series and generated two sequels, *Logan's World* (1977) and *Logan's Search* (1980). Nolan has also written numerous fantasy short stories which like 'My Name is Dolly' have attracted considerable praise. This story was selected for *The Year's Best Fantasy* in 1988.

SOMETHING TO READ

Philip Pullman

The history of wizardry was put down on paper many years ago in books like The Wizard Unvisored *which I mentioned in 'The World of Wizardry'. Apart from such volumes, though, there have been lots of fictitious works such as* The Necronomicon, *a volume of black magic created by H. P. Lovecraft and referred to in several of his short stories;* The Book of Gramarye *featured in* The Dark is Rising (1973) *by Susan Cooper; and all those magical titles like* Necrotelecomnicon *(aka* Liber Paginarum Fulvarum) *written by Achmed the Mad and to be found among the 90,000 volumes in the library at the Unseen University in Terry Pratchett's* Discworld *novels. Hogwarts, too, has a library packed with an A–Z of wonderful titles ranging from Bathilda Bagshot's* A History of Magic *through* Standard Book of Spells (Grade 1) *by Miranda Goshawk,* The Dark Forces: A Guide to Self-Protection *by Quentin Trimble, and that much-consulted classic tome.* Magical Theory *by Adelbert Waffling. Annabel, the girl in this next story, is obsessed with books. She only really feels at home in the school library. In fact, to her books are more real than people. When she goes to a school dance all her inclinations are telling her to read a book rather than mess around with the boys. But the magic spell of words is to take on a whole new meaning for Annabel*

*when she slips away from the seething mass of the dance
floor . . .*

*   *   *

Annabel wandered along the unlit corridor towards
the school library, touching the wallpaper lightly.
There was one patch by the secretary's door where
it was torn, and she had to skim over that bit without
touching the bare plaster, or else she'd have to go
right back to the corner and start again. One day
she'd had to do it no less than four times, and she'd
been late for Science as a result, and had had to
clean out the stick insects.

She paused in the lobby, where the noise of the
school disco was fainter, and read all the notices
for the fifteenth time before looking out through
the glass doors. It was nearly dark. The remains of
the day were staining the sky red over the roofs
of the houses on the estate; little solid clouds
coloured like lemon, butter, and apricot floated even
higher up, against a background of navy blue. Annabel stood there with one hand on the glass and
looked out at them, like a teacher watching the playground.

Suddenly she became aware of a group of boys
standing around a motorbike in the school gateway.
She didn't recognize the one with the helmet, but
the others were in her class, and she opened the door
and called, 'You boys! You ought to be inside!'

They looked away and said nothing, but the boy
with the helmet said a rude word and the others
laughed. She shook her head. Boys like that ought

to be punished, but no one seemed to want to punish them.

She turned away and wandered across to the trophy cabinet. Nothing had been moved in there since 1973, no new names added to the tarnished silver cups and shields. It was a relic of the days when this had been a Grammar School. Annabel sometimes used to long to be back there, to be a pupil in those days, to see her name inscribed on the Edith Butler Shield for Dramatic Recitation, for example. But those times were gone.

She could see her reflection in the glass. She stood up a little straighter and tugged at the waist of her dress, pulling it down. It was too short; she had told them it was too short. It was dark green with a frilly white collar which was already, she thought, coming undone at the back. Why had they made her come? Her taste in music, as they well knew, was for the classics. No boy would want to dance with her, and she had no particular friends to talk to, even supposing you could talk with the music that loud. The whole experience would be *purgatorial*, she'd said passionately.

After a moment she wandered out of the lobby past the Assembly Hall and tried the door of the library. She knew it would be locked, but she felt a wave of bitter disappointment just the same. The one place in the school where she felt at home, and they locked it ... And to make it worse, there was the latest novel by Iris Murdoch on the New Aquisitions shelf. Annabel had read all her others; she sometimes felt that Iris Murdoch had written *her*. She was longing to get her hands on this one, but the Sixth Form had first choice. As if any of them wanted to read it anyway! She could see it from here, tantalizingly close.

Annabel read so much it was like a disease. When she didn't have a book in front of her, her eyes flickered restlessly all around, searching for print, and when they found it, she made for it with the single-minded intensity of a drug-addict making for the deadly white powder. She had always read: it was how she measured her life. When she was five, she had read Dr Seuss; at seven she had gone on to Dick King-Smith and Helen Cresswell; by the age of ten she was reading Diana Wynne-Jones and Susan Cooper; and now at fourteen she was reading books for adults. Reading? Gulping down, rather, like those strange deep-sea fishes, all vast expanding mouth with a little ribbon of body trailing behind.

Anyone watching her would have thought that she actually wanted to consume the books physically. She took a fierce gloating private pleasure in opening a new book, in hearing the crackle of the binding, in smelling the paper, in riffling through the pages, in slowly sliding off the jacket; and while she read, her hands were never still: her thumbs would move back and forth, feeling the smoothness of the paper under them; her fingers would explore the mysteries of the hollow spine. Paperbacks were all right, but they broke easily. It was hardbacks that she coveted.

Yes, she was different from other people, but what did that matter? Other people were shadows. It was books that were real. But her parents had formed the idea that she ought to get out more—make friends, talk to people—and they'd made her come to this disco in order to promote her social development. So here she was, drifting through the empty school while the hideous music thumped in the background. If only she had a book, she could sit quietly somewhere and read it. If she had a book she wouldn't get in anyone's way. She wouldn't bother anyone. Why did they bother her with their discos and their social development? Who needed social development when they had something to read? It would serve them right if she killed herself. And haunted them. If she was a ghost, she could read as much as she liked.

Someone ran shouting down the corridor, and Annabel sighed. Then she pursed her lips ruefully and shook her head. She caught sight of her reflection in the library door and tried the expression again, but it was too dim to see clearly.

What was the time? She peered closely at the gold watch on her thin wrist. It was a family heirloom; it had belonged to her great-aunt, who'd published a book of her reminiscences of life in East Africa, and Annabel was very proud of it. In the faint light from the end of the corridor she saw that it said half past eight. That meant—she counted it off on her fingers—eight forty-one, since she'd set it exactly at six and it lost a minute every quarter of an hour. Ages till the disco finished, then. Where else could she go? Everywhere was locked. Sighing, she touched the library door again and wandered towards the gym where the disco was being held, since there was nothing else to do. The noise of the music—if you could call it music—thudded brutally as she got closer. She took a deep breath, pushed open the gym door, and walked inside.

The noise was appalling, and so was the heat. They'd rigged up some coloured lights that flashed in time with the music, but apart from them the place was in darkness. It seemed like a suburb of hell, thought Annabel, inhabited by wild spirits who leapt up and down shrieking. It *must* be hell. She peered around resignedly. There was Mr Carter the PE teacher, dancing energetically, or *bopping*, as she supposed they call it. And wasn't that Miss Andrews over there? She was wearing a rather revealing dress and a lot more make-up than she normally wore, but it was the English teacher nevertheless. Annabel made for her automatically.

'Hello, Annabel!' Miss Andrews shouted. 'I didn't think you were coming.'

Annabel made a face. Then she said 'This is like Book Two of *Paradise Lost.*'

'What? I can't hear you?'

'I said this is like Book Two of *Paradise Lost!*'

'Is it? Why aren't you dancing?'

Annabel gave a helpless shrug. She didn't think the teacher could have heard her properly. Then one of the older boys tapped Miss Andrews on the shoulder and jerked his head at the dance floor, and she nodded enthusiastically and went to join him. Annabel felt betrayed.

Someone shouted in her ear, and she winced.

'D'you want to dance?' came the shout again.

She turned to look at the speaker. It was a boy from her class called Tim. He was a decent enough boy, very ordinary, slightly plump; didn't read much.

Why was he asking her to dance? Was he making fun of her? There couldn't be any other reason.

She curled her lip and said 'Whatever for?'

That took him aback. He stood there looking embarrassed.

'Well . . . I just thought I'd ask,' he said. 'That's all.'

'Oh, that's all. I see. Did you think I'd enjoy dancing with you? Touching you, perhaps? Squirming and writhing and grunting? Do you think I want to look like *those* people? No, thank you. I'd rather die.'

He had nothing to say. Finally he blinked and turned away. She might have felt triumphant, but something else had already come into her mind, making her flush with guilty pleasure.

She had remembered where she'd left a book!

True, it wasn't a novel; in fact it was a handbook about collecting and polishing semi-precious gemstones. But it was something to read. She'd got it out of the library on Tuesday afternoon, just before Games, and put it in her PE bag, which was still hanging on her peg. She left the gym at once, breathing fast, and made straight for the cloakrooms.

It was dark, but she found her peg easily enough, and fumbled through the damp-smelling towel and clammy gym shoes till her fingers met the precious spine of the book. She hauled it out and pressed it to her breast. Now, where could she sit and read without being disturbed?

The moonlight outside the windows was bright enough to read by, surely. And it wasn't cold at all. She could go to the swimming-pool: no one would want to go there.

Clutching the book to her side, she hurried through the corridors to the front entrance and slipped out as quietly as a shadow and around the side of the school. There was a hedge around the swimming-pool, and a light high up on the school wall above it, just in case the moonlight wasn't enough. Everything was perfect. Even the hedge looked right: like a maze in a formal garden, a maze with a secret pool, hidden away, bathed in stately moonlight, where she could sit and read for ever . . .

She felt for the door, a two-metre-high piece of solid lapped cedar panelling, and nearly stamped with dismay when she found it locked. But she was too determined now to give up. Throwing her book over the door, to make it impossible to retreat, she leapt for the top, grabbed it, hauled herself up and jumped heavily down on the other side.

Panting with pleasure, she felt for the shoe that had come off, pushed back the hair that was hanging lopsidedly over her face, and stood up with the book safe in her hand. Her dress was rucked up, and she hauled it down absently. She was alone and the moon was shining. Everything was silver except for the shiny black water in the pool; even the dull square paving-stones looked soft, worn, antique—like real stone and not concrete.

And no one here but her! That was the best thing of all.

She turned slowly around, imagining a long silk gown fluttering loosely as she moved. She raised her left arm to see how the gold watch caught the moon-light, and thought how slender the arm seemed, how graceful even . . .

But she was already more interested in the book than in fantasies about her own appearance. Kicking off her shoes, she sat down at the edge of the pool and lowered her feet gingerly into the cold water, watching the moon's reflection shake itself like a jelly and little by little gather itself together in one piece. As soon as it was whole again she opened the book. If she held it fairly close it was possible to make out the words. Eyes wide, head bent low, she began to read. A moment later, there was a rustling in the hedge. A girl's voice spoke quietly, and someone giggled.

Annabel sat absolutely still. She was furious: she knew what they were up to. Instead of replying, she bent closer to her book and hunched her shoulders. How dare they?

'Annabel!' said the same voice. It came from somewhere nearby.

Annabel took no notice. There was a whispered exchange, and another giggle.

'*Annabel!*' said the girl again.

Annabel put her hands over her ears.

'Ah, leave her, Linda,' she heard clearly in another voice: a boy's.

'No! I don't want her getting in the way. She can go somewhere else.'

Annabel recognized the voice, having heard the name. Linda was a girl in her class—pretty and popular and very nearly illiterate, as far as Annabel could tell. Annabel pressed her hands tighter, hunched her shoulders closer, glared at the book more intently than ever.

The hedge rustled again and the two figures

stepped out, the boy more reluctantly than the girl. Linda stepped off the grass on to the paved surround of the pool and walked up to Annabel, stopping about a metre away. Annabel pretended to take no notice.

'Annabel, get lost,' the girl said. 'Go somewhere else. We was here first.'

Annabel couldn't resist.

'We *were* here first,' she corrected her. 'I'm surprised to hear you still making that mistake. In any case, I'm busy reading. I hardly think I'm interrupting—'

'Oh, don't bother, Linda,' the boy groaned, and now Annabel recognized him as well. He was called Ian, and she gathered that many of the girls thought him attractive. 'She won't listen. Leave her alone.'

'No, I won't,' said Linda. 'We come out here to mind our own business. She only come out here to get in the way. She can go and read her book anywhere, can't she? Why'd she want to come and get in the way?'

'I am not in the way,' said Annabel.

'If I think you're in the way, you *are* in the way.'

'I wonder whether you had considered the rightness of what you were doing before coming in here yourself,' Annabel said. 'If I were you I should go back to the disco and behave myself. I don't know what your parents—'

'I don't *believe* this!' said Linda. With a little fret of temper she stamped closer, right up against Annabel's shoulder. Annabel could smell her scent and the warm smell of her flesh, and wrinkled her nose before turning back to the book.

Ian hung back, unhappy. Linda nudged Annabel hard with her knee.

'Go on, get lost! All you want to do is read, so go and read somewhere else! No one asked you here! Just get lost!'

Annabel looked up at her coldly. Linda's eyes were bright, her breast was moving as she breathed quickly, the skin of her bare arms was gleaming smoothly in the moonlight.

'Certainly not,' said Annabel. 'I have every right to be here.'

'*I have every right to be here!*' Linda jeered, imitating Annabel's precise voice.

'She ain't going to move, Linda,' said Ian.

And Annabel hadn't moved an inch. The moon was still intact in the water, her hands still held the book on her lap.

But Linda had other ideas. She nudged Annabel again with her knee, harder this time, and the movement shook Annabel's feet in the water. The ripples slowly trailed out towards the moon.

'I can't stand you,' said Linda. 'You're a snob.'

'I am not,' said Annabel. 'A snob is a person who apes the manners of those above them in society. It's not what you think it is at all. If you look it up in the dictionary—'

'Why can't you talk like everyone else? You stupid cow! Are you going to move or what?'

'I decline. And in fact, if you don't go back to the disco at once, I shall tell—'

Before she could say any more, Linda reached down and snatched the book from her hands.

'What are you *doing?*' Annabel cried, and began to

struggle up, but Linda had flung the book out across the swimming pool. It fluttered like a wounded bird, and hit the water to float dumbly a few metres from the side.

'Oh! That's a *library* book!' said Annabel wildly. 'It's not even *mine*!'

She knelt down at the edge and bent low, reaching out to try and paddle the water towards her. Linda turned away and stamped in disgust.

'Ian!' Annabel cried. 'You've got to help! It's too far for me to reach ... where do they keep the bamboo pole? Go and get it! Quick!'

He didn't move. Annabel leant out a little further. The book was bobbing lightly on the water and floating further away. She stood up and ran the few steps to Linda in a frenzy of anger and panic. Seizing Linda's shoulder, she shook it hard.

'Get that book! You just go and get it out of the water! How dare you treat a literary work like that, you barbarian! You illiterate savage!'

Linda, alarmed and angry, turned and shoved Annabel's hand away. Then Annabel hit her. The slap cracked loudly over the water. Breathless with astonishment, Linda gathered her wits and tried to strike back, but Annabel grabbed her hair and tried to force her into the pool. There was a moment of struggle, and someone shouted, and then Annabel herself lost her balance and, with a faint cry, fell in.

She sank at once. Swimming was not one of her strong points, but she knew that the human body tended to float; she could only suppose that the green dress was pulling her down.

She touched the bottom and kicked two or three

times till she began to drift up again. At one point she felt the floating book with her fingertips, but she couldn't get hold of it, and then she was at the surface again. It wasn't at all cold.

She opened her eyes to see something amusing, as she thought: Ian and Linda kneeling side by side, peering down into the water with guilt on their faces. It occurred to her that more time had passed than she had thought.

And then she realized that she was dead. Well, wouldn't that serve them right!

There was no doubt about it. She got out of the pool and stood shivering beside them as her body floated up clumsily. Ian put his arms around Linda, and then changed his mind and reached out towards the body.

'It weren't my fault, Ian!' Linda said. 'You saw! She tried to push me in . . . Oh, this is horrible! What we gonna do?'

'She just fell in,' Ian said stupidly. 'You never pushed her . . . I better pull her out, what d'you reckon? Oh, God! Here, we better get Mr Carter. 'You go and tell him and I'll . . . I dunno. Quick, go on.'

'How'm I going to . . .' Linda gestured helplessly at the hedge.

'Oh, God! I dunno! Same way we come in! Go on!'

Linda ran to the hedge at the end and shoved herself at it blindly, while Ian paddled the water, trying to make Annabel's body drift towards him.

'I think the bamboo pole's over by the pump,' said Annabel, but Ian took no notice. 'If you grab the edge of my skirt you might be able to pull me a bit closer.'

It was useless. He couldn't hear her at all.

'I don't think it'll float for long,' said Annabel more loudly. 'Probably my lungs are still full of water, which will increase the specific gravity of the body. You'd better be quick before it sinks. I'm not in any position to help at the moment. And it was entirely your fault, the pair of you.'

It was no different, being dead. They still took no notice. She felt desolated, but that was nothing new either. You might have thought it would be quite interesting to be dead, at least at first, but it was worse than being alive. She didn't even want the book much any more.

Ian had given up trying to get her to float towards him, and was standing irresolutely by the hedge. He didn't look at the body. Annabel thought he looked frightened.

Then—it was like the feeling returning to a limb that had gone to sleep—she began to realize what it meant. She was dead. She was shut out for ever. Her future was snuffed out; the books she was going to write, her career as an author—it would never happen. She started to cry.

There was a sound of running feet and someone fumbling with the padlock, and then the gate crashed open. Mr Carter came in with a rush and took one look at the pool and at Ian.

'Haven't you done *anything*?' he said.

He dived straight in, sending water splashing right through where Annabel was standing. He surfaced by the body, gasping, and lifted her head clear, then heaved her on to her back and towed her to the side.

'I'll lift her,' he said to Ian. 'You get hold and pull her out. Roll her over the edge. Come on, move!'

Ian hurried to do as he was told. Annabel hovered nearby, feeling irritated by their clumsiness. They seemed to be doing it on purpose to make her look ridiculous; they let her lank body droop awkwardly across the edge of the pool, streaming water from nose and mouth, as the sodden dark green dress bound her legs together. Ian hauled at one arm.

'For God's sake, boy, take hold properly!' Mr Carter said, gasping with cold. 'You'll dislocate her shoulder! Take her up gently . . .'

Annabel felt tears again. She looked down mistily at the poor dank thing sprawled wetly on the concrete, and saw Mr Carter kneel beside her, take her head in his hands, and kiss her. She began to sob and moved away from the pool. There was a crowd gathering at the gate: open mouths, cruel wide eyes. She couldn't bear it.

She went back into the school and sat in the lobby. The disco music was still thudding from the gym, and it was clear that most of the kids had no idea that anything unusual had happened. Annabel didn't know what to do. What do you do when you're dead? Where do you go?

She felt bitterly frustrated. She wanted to explain whose fault it was, but no one would hear. She watched as things happened: Mr Carter carried her body in and laid it in the Medical Room; Miss Andrews rang her parents; the police arrived, and then the ambulance; all the kids were sent home except for Ian and Linda, who were told to wait in the Head's study. Annabel didn't want to sit with them, so she went into the Medical Room to be with her body.

It had never been attractive, and now it was grotesque. One eye was open and the other half-shut; her mouth hung wide and wet; her legs and arms were stiff and awkward, like a puppet's. How dare they leave it like that? They must have done it on purpose. When she heard her mother and father arrive, she left the room. It would have been too embarrassing.

Instead she went along to the gym, where the lights were still switched on, and looked at the table where they'd been operating the disco. It was a complicated machine they'd hired for the night, with two turn-tables and a microphone and all kinds of switches. The records were strewn across another table nearby, and Annabel went over to read the labels. She was rather disappointed at how little information there was on them; she'd had the impression that record sleeves were covered in print. Perhaps that was just classical records.

Eventually the Head arrived and spoke to her parents. Annabel watched it all distantly. She still hadn't worked out what she ought to do. It was a puzzle.

When everyone had gone, and rather inconsiderately turned the lights out, she felt her way back to the lobby. She trailed her hand over the wallpaper, skimming the torn patch by the Secretary's door, but she couldn't feel it: she missed it twice and had to go back.

Then she noticed something very curious indeed.

She could put her hand right through the wall. In the dim light from the glass front of the lobby, she seemed to be leaning on the wall with a stump. How peculiar!

After trying it gingerly once or twice, she stepped a little closer and tried to walk through. Without the slightest difficulty she found herself in the Secretary's office. It was darker in there, but she could still see quite clearly; perhaps it was never quite dark when you were dead.

She did it several times. It was really quite extraordinary, and yet it felt perfectly natural. Why, she could go anywhere . . .

She could get into the library! At last she could find something to read!

She turned and ran gleefully down the corridor. The whole library all to herself, and no one to tell her to go somewhere else or stop reading or do her homework or make conversation! It was almost worth being dead for that.

She stepped through the library door and paused a moment, with a little shaky sigh of satisfaction, gloating like a cat with a mouse. All those worlds that lay there on the shelves—all hers! Where could she start?

The new Iris Murdoch.

Licking her lips, Annabel moved towards the book greedily, reached for it, and missed.

That was clumsy. She tried again, and missed again. What was the matter with her?

She reached out tremblingly to touch the book, and her hand went right through it.

Then, all at once, the truth dawned. She would

never be able to pick it up. She'd never be able to open it. In desperation she tried another book, with the same result.

She ran to another shelf, trying not to believe what was happening. She plunged her arms, her face, her whole body into shelf after shelf, trying to find something solid in the airy semblance of books that hung all around her; she even felt herself biting at them, trying to get at them that way, but her hands and teeth and arms met nothing at all—nothing but empty space. Finally, trembling, she stood still in horror.

All the books in the world were closed. Hundreds, thousands, millions of books, and all closed, and they would always remain closed. She would never feel that fierce joy of holding a book, smelling it, running her fingers through the pages, pressing her face to it. She would never be able to *read* . . .

Unless she stood behind someone and read over their shoulder.

But when she thought of the sort of books they *chose* . . . and how slowly and reluctantly they read, how eager they were to stop and throw the book down . . . face down . . .

Oh, it would be *purgatorial!*

Hadn't she said that before, about the disco?

But this was worse than any disco. Purgatory had been bad enough, but this was hell. And now she knew precisely what hell meant. It meant having all the books in the world, for ever, and nothing to read.

*   *   *

PHILIP PULLMAN was a teacher at three middle schools in Oxford during the 1970s and early 1980s, during which time he won a publisher's competition with his first novel. He has subsequently written a number of popular fantasy stories for younger readers including *Count Karlstein; or, The Ride of the Demon Huntsman* (1982) and *Spring-Heeled Jack* (1989), but achieved international recognition as a writer for all ages with the first of *His Dark Materials* series, *Northern Lights*, which won the Carnegie Award in 1996. Inspired by Milton's *Paradise Lost*, the book introduces twelve-year-old Lyra Silvertongue who lives in a magical world where every individual has their own 'daemon' that evil forces are forever attempting to remove by 'intercision'. The spectres, ghosts, angels and witches who appeared in this groundbreaking book and returned in the second, *The Subtle Knife* (1997), are certainly unique in contemporary fiction.

CAROL ONEIR'S
HUNDREDTH DREAM

Diana Wynne Jones

All wizards have been proud of their ability to predict the future, read the signs and interpret dreams. Among the real wizards who were particularly good at this were Merlin, Michael Scot and Roger Bacon. In fiction, the wizards of Discworld who boast these skills include the Arch-Astronomer of Krull, the youthful Igneous Cutwell and Granny Weatherwax, 'The Greatest Witch on Discworld'. In Harry Potter and the Philosopher's Stone, *of course, Professor McGonagall displays amazing foresight when he says of the young wizard-to-be, 'He'll be famous—a legend . . . every child in our world will know his name.' An awful lot of people also know Carol Oneir the central character in this final story. She's incredibly clever and ever since the age of seven she has been able to control her dreams. This has made her famous as the author of lots of books and comics and many other pieces of merchandise. Then just as Carol is about to have her one hundredth dream . . . nothing happens. It is a crisis that can mean the end of her career until her dad has the smart idea of getting in touch with one of his old school friends, the wizard, Chrestomanci. He's an enchanter with nine lives who lives in a world next door to ours where magic is as common as music and the place is full of people making it like witches, sorcerers, conjurors and magicians. Because his magic is far stronger than theirs, Chrestomanci—it's pronounced KREST-OH-MAN-SEE—often has to intervene in their affairs. So who better to solve the mystery of why Carol Oneir has lost her power to dream . . .*

*   *   *

Carol Oneir was the world's youngest best-selling dreamer. The newspapers called her the Infant Genius. Her photograph appeared regularly in all the daily papers and monthly magazines, either sitting alone in an armchair looking soulful, or nestling lovingly against her mama.

Mama was very proud of Carol. So were Carol's publishers, Wizard Reverie Ltd. They marketed her product in big bright blue genie jars tied with cherry-coloured satin ribbon; but you could also buy the Carol *Oneir Omnibus Pillow*, bright pink and heart shaped, *Carol's Dreamie Comics*, the *Carol Oneir Dream Hatband*, the *Carol Oneir Charm Bracelet* and a half a hundred other spin-offs.

Carol had discovered at the age of seven that she was one of those lucky people who can control what they dream about, and then loosen the dream in their minds so that a competent wizard can spin it off and bottle it for other people to enjoy. Carol loved dreaming. She had made no less than ninety-nine full-length dreams. She loved all the attention she got and all the expensive things her mama was able to buy for her. So it was a terrible blow to her when she lay down one night to start dreaming her hundredth dream and nothing happened at all.

It was a terrible blow to Mama too, who had just ordered a champagne breakfast to celebrate *Carol's Dream Century*. Wizard Reverie Ltd were just as upset as Mama. Their nice Mr Ploys got up in the middle of the night and came down to Surrey by the milk train. He soothed Mama, and he soothed Carol, and he persuaded Carol to lie down and try to dream again. But Carol still could not dream. She tried every day for the following week, but she had no dreams at all, not even the kind of dreams ordinary people have.

The only person who took it calmly was Dad. He went fishing as soon as the crisis started. Mr Ploys and Mama took Carol to all the best doctors, in case Carol was overtired or ill. But she wasn't. So Mama took Carol up to Harley Street to consult Herman Mindelbaum the famous mind wizard. But Mr Mindelbaum could find nothing wrong either. He said Carol's mind was in perfect order and that her self-confidence was rather surprisingly high, considering.

In the car going home, Mama wept and Carol sobbed. Mr Ploys said frantically, 'Whatever happens, we mustn't let a *hint* of this get to the newspapers!' But of course it was too late. Next day the papers all had headlines saying CAROL ONEIR SEES MIND SPECIALIST and IS CAROL ALL DREAMED OUT? Mama burst into tears again, and Carol could not eat any breakfast.

Dad came home from fishing later that day to find reporters sitting in rows on the front steps. He prodded his way politely through them with his fishing rod, saying, 'There is nothing to get excited about. My daughter is just very tired, and we're taking her to Switzerland for a rest.' When he finally got indoors, he said, 'We're in luck. I've managed to arrange for Carol to see an expert.'

'Don't be silly, dear. We saw Mr Mindelbaum yesterday,' Mama sobbed.

'I know, dear. But I said an expert, not a specialist,' said Dad. 'You see, I used to be at school with Chrestomanci—once, long ago, when we were both younger than Carol. In fact, he lost his first life because I hit him round the head with a cricket bat. Now, of course, being a nine-lifed enchanter, he's a great deal more important than Carol is, and I had a lot of trouble getting hold of him. I was afraid he wouldn't want to remember me, but he did. He said he'd see Carol. The snag is, he's on holiday in the South of France and he doesn't want the resort filling with newspapermen—'

'I'll see to all that,' Mr Ploys cried joyfully. 'Chrestomanci! Mr Oneir, I'm *awed*. I'm struck dumb!'

Two days later, Carol and her parents and Mr Ploys boarded first class sleepers in Calais on the Swiss Orient Express. The reporters boarded it too, in second class sleepers and third class seats, and they were joined by French and German reporters standing in the corridors. The crowded train rattled away through France until, in the middle of the night, it came to Strasbourg, where a lot of shunting always went on. Carol's sleeper, with Carol and her parents asleep in it, was shunted off and hitched to the back of the Riviera Golden Arrow, and the Swiss Orient went on to Zurich without her.

Mr Ploys went to Switzerland with it. He told Carol that, although he was really a dream wizard, he had skill enough to keep the reporters thinking Carol was still on the train. 'If Chrestomanci wants to be private,' he said, 'it could cost me my job if I let one of these near him.'

By the time the reporters discovered the deception, Carol and her parents had arrived in the seaside resort of Teignes on the French Riviera. There Dad— not without one or two wistful looks at the casino— unpacked his rods and went fishing. Mama and Carol took a horse-drawn cab up the hill to the private villa where Chrestomanci was staying.

They dressed in their best for the appointment. Neither of them had met anyone before who was more important than Carol. Carol wore ruched blue satin the same colour as her genie bottles, with no less than three hand-embroidered lace petticoats underneath it. She had on matching button boots and a blue ribbon in her carefully curled hair, and she carried a blue satin parasol. She also wore her diamond heart pendant, her brooch that said CAROL in diamonds, her two sapphire bracelets, and all six of her gold bangles. Her blue satin bag had diamond clasps in the shape of two Cs. Mama was even more magnificent in a cherry-coloured Paris gown, a pink hat, and all her emeralds.

They were shown up to a terrace by a rather plain lady who, as Mama whispered to Carol behind her fan, was really rather overdressed for a servant. Carol envied Mama her fan.

There were so many stairs to the terrace that she was too hot to speak when they got there. She let Mama exclaim at the wonderful view. You could see the sea and the beach, and look into the streets of

Teignes from here. As Mama said, the casino looked charming and the golf links so peaceful. On the other side, the villa had its own private swimming pool. This was full of splashing, screaming children, and, to Carol's mind, it rather spoiled the view.

Chrestomanci was sitting reading in a deck chair. He looked up and blinked a little as they came. Then he seemed to remember who they were and stood up with great politeness to shake hands. He was wearing a beautifully tailored natural-silk suit. Carol saw at a glance that it had cost at least as much as Mama's Paris gown. But her first thought on seeing Chrestomanci was, Oh my! He's twice as good-looking as Francis! She pushed that thought down quickly and trod it under. It belonged to the thoughts she never even told Mama. But it meant that she rather despised Chrestomanci for being quite so tall and for having hair so black and such flashing dark eyes. She knew he was going to be no more help than Mr Mindelbaum, and Mr Mindelbaum had reminded her of Melville.

Mama meanwhile was holding Chrestomanci's hand between both of hers and saying, 'Oh, sir! This is so good of you to interrupt your holiday on our account! But when even Mr Mindelbaum couldn't find out what's stopping her dreams—'

'Not at all,' Chrestomanci said, wrestling for his hand rather. 'To be frank, I was intrigued by a case even Mindelbaum couldn't fathom.' He signalled to the serving lady who had brought them to the terrace. 'Millie, do you think you could take Mrs . . . er . . . O'Dear downstairs while I talk to Carol?'

'There's no need for that, sir,' Mama said, smiling.

'I always go everywhere with my darling. Carol knows I'll sit quite quietly and not interrupt.'

'No wonder Mindelbaum got nowhere,' Chrestomanci murmured.

Then—Carol, who prided herself on being very observant, was never quite sure how it happened—Mama was suddenly not on the terrace any more. Carol herself was sitting in a deck chair facing Chrestomanci in his deck chair, listening to Mama's voice floating up from below somewhere. 'I never let Carol go anywhere alone. She's my one ewe lamb . . .'

Chrestomanci leaned back comfortably and crossed his elegant legs. 'Now,' he said, 'be kind enough to tell me exactly what you do when you make a dream.'

This was something Carol had done hundreds of times by now. She smiled graciously and began, 'I get a feeling in my head first, which means a dream is ready to happen. Dreams come when they will, you know, and there is no stopping them or putting them off. So I tell Mama, and we go up to my boudoir, where she helps me to get settled on the special couch Mr Ploys had made for me. Then Mama sets the spin-off spool turning and tiptoes away, and I drop off to sleep to the sound of it gently humming and whirling. Then the dream takes me . . .'

Chrestomanci did not take notes like Mr Mindelbaum and the reporters. He did not nod at her encouragingly the way Mr Mindelbaum had. He simply stared vaguely out to sea. Carol thought that the least he might do was to tell those children in the pool to keep quiet. The screaming and splashing was so loud that she almost had to shout. Carol thought he was being very inconsiderate, but she kept on.

'I have learned not to be frightened and to go where the dream takes me. It is like a voyage of discovery—'

'When is this?' Chrestomanci interrupted in an offhand sort of way. 'Does this dreaming happen at night?'

'It can happen at any time,' said Carol. 'If a dream is ready, I can go to my couch and sleep during the day.'

'How very useful,' murmured Chrestomanci. 'So you can put up your hand in a dull lesson and say "Please can I be excused to go and dream?" Do they let you go home?'

'I ought to have explained,' Carol said, keeping her dignity with an effort, 'that Mama arranges lessons for me at home so that I can dream any time I need to. It's like a voyage of discovery, sometimes in caves underground, sometimes in palaces in the clouds—'

'Yes. And how long do you dream for? Six hours? Ten minutes?' Chrestomanci interrupted again.

'About half an hour,' said Carol. 'Sometimes in the clouds, or maybe in the southern seas. I never know where I will go or whom I will meet on my journey—'

'Do you finish a whole dream in half an hour?' Chrestomanci interrupted yet again.

'Of course not. Some of my dreams last for more than three hours,' Carol said. 'As for the people I meet, they are strange and wonderful—'

'So you dream in half-hour stretches,' said Chrestomanci. 'And I suppose you have to take a dream up

again exactly where you left it at the end of the half
hour before.'

'Obviously,' said Carol. 'People must have told
you—I can *control* my dreams. And I do my best
work in regular half-hour stints. I wish you wouldn't
keep interrupting, when I'm doing my best to tell
you!'

Chrestomanci turned his face from the sea and
looked at her. He seemed surprised. 'My dear young
lady, you are *not* doing your best to tell me. I do read
the papers, you know. You are giving me precisely
the same flannel you gave *The Times* and the *Croydon
Gazette* and the *People's Monthly*, and doubtless poor
Mindelbaum as well. You are telling me your dreams
come unbidden—but you have one for half an hour
every day—and that you never know where you'll go
in them or what will happen—but you can control
your dreams perfectly. That can't all be true, can it?'

Carol slid the bangles up and down her arm and
tried to keep her temper. It was difficult to do when
the sun was so hot and the noise coming from that
pool so loud. She thought seriously of demoting Melville and making Chrestomanci into the villain in her
next dream—until she remembered that there might
not *be* a next dream unless Chrestomanci helped her.
'I don't understand,' she said.

'Let's talk about the dreams themselves then,' said
Chrestomanci. He pointed down the terrace steps to
the blue, blue water of the pool. 'There you see my
ward, Janet. She's the fair-haired girl the others are
just pushing off the diving board. She loves your
dreams. She has all ninety-nine of them—though I
am afraid Julia and the boys are very contemptuous

about it. They say your dreams are slush and all exactly the same.'

Naturally Carol was deeply hurt that anyone could call her dreams slush, but she knew better than to say so. She smiled graciously down at the large splash which was all she could see of Janet.

'Janet is hoping to meet you later,' said Chrestomanci. Carol's smile broadened. She loved meeting admirers. 'When I heard you were coming,' Chrestomanci said, 'I borrowed Janet's latest Omnibus Pillow.' Carol's smile narrowed a bit. Chrestomanci did not seem the kind of person who would enjoy her dreams at all.

'I enjoyed it rather,' Chrestomanci confessed. Carol's smile widened. Well! 'But Julia and the boys are right, you know,' Chrestomanci went on. 'Your happy endings are pretty slushy, and the same sort of things happen in all of them.' Carol's smile narrowed again distinctly at this. 'But they're terribly lively,' Chrestomanci said. 'There's so much action and so many people. I like all those crowds—what your blurbs call your "cast of thousands"—but I must confess I don't find your settings very convincing. That Arabian setting in the ninety-sixth dream was awful, even making allowances for how young you are. On the other hand, your fairground in the latest dream seemed to show the makings of a real gift.'

By this time, Carol's smile was going broad and narrow like the streets of Dublin's Fair City. She was almost caught off guard when Chrestomanci said, 'And though you never appear in your dreams yourself, a number of characters do come in over and over again—in various disguises of course. I make it about five or six main actors in all.'

This was getting far too close to the things Carol never told even Mama. Luckily some reporters had made the same observation. 'This is the way dreams are,' she said. 'And I am only the Seeing Eye.'

'As you told the *Manchester Guardian*,' Chrestomanci agreed, 'if that is what they meant by "Oosung Oyo". I see that must have been a misprint now.' He was looking very vague, to Carol's relief, and did not seem to notice her dismay. 'Now,' he said, 'I suggest the time has come for you to go to sleep and let me see what happened to send your hundredth dream so wrong that you refused to record it.'

'But nothing went wrong!' Carol protested. 'I just didn't dream.'

'So you say,' said Chrestomanci. 'Close your eyes. Feel free to snore if you wish.'

'But . . . but I can't just go to sleep in the middle of a visit!' Carol said. 'And . . . and those children in the pool are making far too much noise.'

Chrestomanci put one hand casually down to the paving of the terrace. Carol saw his arm go up as if he were pulling something up out of the stones. The terrace went quiet. She could see the children splashing below, and their mouths opening and shutting, but not a sound came to her ears. 'Have you run out of excuses now?' he asked.

'They're not excuses. And how are you going to know whether I dream or not without a proper dream-spool and a qualified dream-wizard to read it?' Carol demanded.

'Oh, I daresay I can manage quite well without,'

Chrestomanci remarked. Though he said it in a mild, sleepy sort of way, Carol suddenly remembered that he was a nine-lifed enchanter, and more important than she was. She supposed he thought he was powerful enough on his own. Well, let him. She would humour him. Carol arranged her blue parasol to keep some of the sun off her and settled back in her deck chair, knowing nothing was going to happen . . .

. . . And she was at the fairground, where her ninety-ninth dream had left off. In front of her was a wide space of muddy grass, covered with bits of paper and other rubbish. She could see the Big Wheel in the distance behind some flapping tents and half-dismantled stalls, and another tall thing that seemed to be most of the Helter Skelter tower. The place seemed quite deserted.

'Well *really*!' Carol said. 'They still haven't cleared anything up! What are Martha and Paul *thinking* of?'

As soon as she said that, she clapped her hands guiltily to her mouth and whirled round to make sure that Chrestomanci had not come stalking up behind her. But there was nothing behind her but more dreary, litter-covered grass. Good! Carol thought. I *knew* nobody could come behind the scenes in a Carol Oneir private dream unless I let them! She relaxed. She was boss here. This was part of the things she never even told Mama—though, for a moment, back on the terrace at Teignes, she had been afraid that Chrestomanci was on to her.

The fact was, as Chrestomanci had noticed, Carol did only have six main characters working for her.

There was Francis, tall and fair and handsome, with a beautiful baritone voice, who did all the heroes. He always ended up marrying the gentle but spirited Lucy, who was fair too and very pretty. Then there was Melville, who was thin and dark, with an evil white face, who did all the villains. Melville was so good at being a Baddie that Carol often used him several times in one dream. But he was always the gentleman, which was why polite Mr Mindelbaum had reminded Carol of Melville.

The other three were Bimbo, who was oldish and who did all the Wise Old Men, Pathetic Cripples, and Weak Tyrants; Martha, who was the Older Woman and did the Aunts, Mothers, and Wicked Queens, either straight wicked or with Hearts of Gold; and Paul, who was small and boyish looking. Paul's speciality was the Faithful Boy Assistant, though he did Second Baddie too and tended to get killed quite often in both kinds of parts. Paul and Martha, since they never had very big parts, were supposed to see that the cast of thousands cleared everything up between dreams.

Except that they hadn't this time.

'Paul!' Carol shouted. 'Martha! Where's my cast of thousands?'

Nothing happened. Her voice just went rolling away into emptiness.

'Very well!' Carol called out. 'I shall come and find you, and you won't like it when I do!'

She set off, picking her way disgustedly through the rubbish, toward those flapping tents. It really was too bad of them, she thought, to let her down like this, when she had gone to all the trouble of making them up and giving them a hundred disguises, and had made them as famous as she was herself, in a way. As Carol thought this, her bare foot came down in a melted ice cream. She jumped back with a shudder and found she was, for some reason, wearing a bathing suit like the children in Chrestomanci's pool.

'Oh really!' she said crossly. She remembered now that her other attempt at a hundredth dream had gone like this too, up to the point where she had scrapped it. Anyone would think this was the kind of dream ordinary people had. It wouldn't even make a decent *Hatband* dream. This time, with a sternly controlled effort, she made herself wear her blue button boots and the blue dress with all its petticoats underneath. It was hotter like that, but it showed that she was in charge. And she marched on, until she came to the flapping tents.

Here it nearly came like a common dream again. Carol walked up and down among empty tents and collapsed stalls, under the great framework of the Big Wheel and repeatedly past the topless Helter Skelter tower, past roundabout after empty roundabout, without seeing a soul.

It was only her stern annoyance that kept her going until she did see someone, and then she nearly went straight past him, thinking he was one of the dummies from the Waxworks Show. He was sitting on a box beside a painted organ from a roundabout, staring. Perhaps some of the cast of thousands did work as dummies when necessary, Carol thought. She had no idea really. But this one was fair, so that meant he was a Goodie and generally worked with Francis.

'Hey, you!' she said. 'Where's Francis?'

He gave her a dull, unfinished sort of look. 'Rhubarb,' he said. 'Abracadabra.'

'Yes, but you're not doing a crowd scene now,' Carol told him. 'I want to know where my Main Characters are.'

The man pointed vaguely beyond the Big Wheel. 'In their quarters,' he said. 'Committee meeting.' So Carol set off that way. She had barely gone two steps when the man called out from behind her. 'Hey you! Say thank you!'

How rude! thought Carol. She turned and glared at him. He was now drinking out of a very strong-smelling green bottle. 'You're drunk!' she said. 'Where did you get that? I don't allow real drink in my dreams.'

'Name's Norman,' said the man. 'Drowning sorrows.'

Carol saw that she was not going to get any sense out of him. So she said 'Thank you,' to stop him shouting after her again and went the way he had pointed. It led her among a huddle of gypsy caravans. Since these all had a blurred cardboard sort of look, Carol went straight past them, knowing they must belong to the cast of thousands. She knew the caravan she wanted would look properly clear and real. And it did. It was more like a tarry black shed on wheels than a caravan, but there was real black smoke pouring out of its rusty iron chimney.

Carol sniffed it. 'Funny. It smells almost like toffee!' But she decided not to give her people any further warning. She marched up the black wooden ladder to the door and flung the door open.

Smoke and heat and the smell of drink and toffee rolled out at her. Her people were all inside, but instead of turning politely to receive their orders as they usually did, none of them at first took any notice of her at all. Francis was sitting at the table playing cards with Martha, Paul, and Bimbo by the light of candles stuck in green bottles. Glasses of strong-smelling drink stood at each of their elbows, but most of the drink smell, to Carol's horror, was coming from the bottle Lucy was drinking out of. Beautiful, gentle Lucy was sitting on a bunk at the back, giggling and nursing a green bottle. As far as Carol could see in the poor light, Lucy's face looked like a gnome's and her hair was what Mama would describe as 'in tetters'. Melville was cooking at the stove near the door. Carol was ashamed to look at him. He was wearing a grubby white apron and smiling a dreamy smile as he stirred his saucepan. Anything less villain-ous was hard to imagine.

'And just what,' said Carol, 'do you think you're all doing?'

At that, Francis turned around enough for her to see that he had not shaved for days. 'Shut that blesh door, can' you!' he said irritably. It was possible he spoke that way because he had a large cigar between his teeth, but Carol feared it was more likely to be because Francis was drunk.

She shut the door and stood in front of it with her arms folded. 'I want an explanation,' she said. 'I'm waiting.'

Paul slapped down his cards and briskly pulled a pile of money toward himself. Then he took the cigar out of his boyish mouth to say, 'And you can go on waiting, unless you've come to negotiate at last. We're on strike.'

'On strike!' said Carol.

'On strike,' Paul said. 'All of us. I brought the cast of thousands out straight after the last dream. We want better working conditions and a bigger slice of the cake.' He gave Carol a challenging and not very pleasant grin and put the cigar back in his mouth— a mouth that was not so boyish, now Carol looked at it closely. Paul was older than she had realised, with little cynical lines all over his face.

'Paul's our shop steward,' Martha said. Martha, to Carol's surprise, was quite young, with reddish hair and a sulky, righteous look. Her voice had a bit of a whine to it when she went on. 'We have our rights, you know. The conditions the cast of thousands have to live in are appalling, and it's one dream straight after another and no free time at all for any of us. And it's not as if we get job satisfaction, either. The rotten parts Paul and I do!'

'Measly walk-ons,' Paul said, busy dealing out cards. 'One of the things we're protesting is being killed almost every dream. The cast of thousands gets gunned down in every final scene, and not only do they get no compensation, they have to get straight up and fight all through the next dream.'

' 'nd never allowsh ush any dthrink,' Bimbo put in. Carol could see he was very drunk. His nose was purple with it, and his white hair looked damp. 'Got shick of coloured water. Had to shteal fruit from Enshanted Garden dream to make firsht wine. Make whishky now. It'sh better.'

'It's not as if you *paid* us anything,' Martha whined.

'We have to take what reward we can get for our services.'

'Then where did you get all that money?' Carol demanded, pointing to the large heap in front of Paul.

'The Arabian treasure scene and so forth,' said Paul. 'Pirates' hoard. Most of it's only painted paper.'

Francis suddenly said, in a loud slurry voice, 'I want recognition. I've been ninety-nine different heroes, but not a word of credit goes on any pillow or jar.' He banged the table. 'Exploitation! That's what it is!'

'Yes, we all want our names on the next dream,' Paul said. 'Melville, give her our list of complaints, will you?'

'Melville's our Strike Committee Secretary,' said Martha.

Francis banged the table again and shouted, '*Melville!*' Then everyone else shouted, 'MELVILLE!' until Melville finally turned round from the stove holding his saucepan in one hand and a sheet of paper in the other.

'I didn't want to spoil my fudge,' Melville said apologetically. He handed the paper to Carol. 'There, my dear. This wasn't my idea, but I didn't wish to let the others down.'

Carol, by this time, was backed against the door, more or less in tears. This dream seemed to be a nightmare. 'Lucy!' she called out desperately. 'Lucy, are you in this too?'

'Don't you disturb her,' said Martha, whom Carol was beginning to dislike very much. 'Lucy's suffered enough. She's had her fill of parts that make her a

plaything and property of men. Haven't you, love?'
she called to Lucy.

Lucy looked up. 'Nobody understands,' she said,
staring mournfully at the wall. 'I hate Francis. And I
always have to marry him and live hap-*hic*-hallipy ever
after.'

This, not surprisingly, annoyed Francis. 'And I hate
you!' he bawled, jumping up as he shouted. The table
went over with a crash, and the glasses, money, cards,
and candles went with it. In the terrifying dark
scramble that followed, the door somehow burst
open behind Carol, and she got herself out through
it as fast as she could . . .

. . . And found herself sitting on a deck chair on the
sunny terrace again. She was holding a paper in one
hand, and her parasol was rolling by her feet. To her
annoyance, someone had spilt a long sticky trickle of
what seemed to be fudge all down her blue dress.

'Tonino! Vieni qui!' somebody called.

Carol looked up to find Chrestomanci trying to
put together a broken deck chair in the midst of a
crowd of people who were all pushing past him and
hurrying away down the terrace steps. Carol could
not think who the people were at first, until she
caught a glimpse of Francis among them, and then
Lucy, who had one hand clutched around her bottle
and the other in the hand of Norman, the man Carol
had first met sitting on a box. The rest of them must
be the cast of thousands, she supposed. She was still
trying to imagine what had happened, when Chrestomanci dropped the broken deck chair and stopped
the very last person to cross the terrace.

'Excuse me, sir,' Chrestomanci said. 'Would you mind explaining a few things before you leave.'

It was Melville, still in his cook's apron, waving smoke away from his saucepan with one long, villainous hand and peering down at his fudge with a very doleful look on his long, villainous face. 'I think it's spoiled,' he said. 'You want to know what happened? Well, I think the cast of thousands started it, around the time Lucy fell in love with Norman, so it may have been Norman's doing to begin with. Anyway, they began complaining that they never got a chance to be real people, and Paul heard them. Paul is very ambitious, you know, and he knew, as we all did, that Francis isn't really cut out to be a hero—'

'No indeed. He has a weak chin,' Chrestomanci agreed.

Carol gasped and was just about to make a protest—which would have been a rather tearful one at that moment—when she recalled that Francis's bristly chin had indeed looked rather small and wobbly under that cigar.

'Oh you shouldn't judge by chins,' said Melville. 'Look at mine—and I'm no more a villain than Francis is a hero. But Francis has his petulant side, and Paul played on that, with the help of Bimbo and his whisky, and Lucy was with Paul anyway because she hated being forced to wear frilly dresses and simper at Francis. She and Norman want to take up farming. And Martha, who is a very frivolous girl to my mind, came in with them because she cannot abide having to clear up the scenery at such short notice. So then they all came to me.'

'And you held out?' asked Chrestomanci.

'All through *The Cripple of Monte Christo* and *The Arabian Knight*,' Melville admitted, ambling across the terrace to park his saucepan on the balustrade. 'I am fond of Carol, you see, and I am quite ready to be three villains at once for her if that is what she wants. But when she started on the Fairground dream straight after *The Tyrant of London Town*, I had to admit that we were all being thoroughly overworked. None of us got any time to be ourselves. Dear me,' he added. 'I think the cast of thousands is preparing to paint the town red.'

Chrestomanci came and leaned on the balustrade to see. 'I fear so,' he said. 'What do you think makes Carol work you all so hard? Ambition?'

There was now such a noise coming from the town that Carol could not resist getting up to look too. Large numbers of the cast of thousands had made straight for the beach. They were joyously racing into the water, pulling little wheeled bathing huts after them, or simply casting their clothes away and plunging in. This was causing quite an outcry from the regular holidaymakers. More outcries came from the main square below the casino, where the cast of thousands had flooded into all the elegant cafés, shouting for ice cream, wine, and frogs' legs.

'It looks rather fun,' said Melville. 'No, not ambition exactly, sir. Say rather that Carol was caught up in success, and her Mama was caught up with her. It is not easy to stop something when one's Mama expects one to go on and on.'

A horse-drawn cab was now galloping along the main street, pursued by shouting, scrambling, excited people. Pursuing these was a little posse of gendarmes. This seemed to be because the white-bearded person in the cab was throwing handfuls of jewels in all directions in the most abandoned way. Arabian jewels and pirates' treasure mostly, Carol thought. She wondered if they would turn out to be glass, or real jewels.

'Poor Bimbo,' said Melville. 'He sees himself as a sort of kingly Santa Claus these days. He has played those parts too often. I think he should retire.'

'And what a pity your Mama told your cab to wait,' Chrestomanci said to Carol. 'Isn't that Francis, Martha and Paul, there? Just going into the casino.'

They were, too. Carol saw them waltzing arm in arm up the marble steps, three people obviously going on a spree.

'Paul,' said Melville, 'tells me he has a system to break the bank.'

'A fairly common delusion,' said Chrestomanci.

'But he can't!' said Carol. 'He hasn't got any real money!' She chanced to look down as she spoke. Her diamond pendant was gone. So was her diamond brooch. Her sapphire bangles and every one of her gold ones were missing. Even the clasps other hand-bag had been torn off. 'They robbed me?' she cried out.

'That would be Martha,' Melville said sadly. 'Remember she picked pockets in *The Tyrant of London Town.*'

'It sounds as if you owed them quite a sum in wages,' Chrestomanci said.

'But what shall I *do*?' Carol wailed. 'How am I going to get everyone back?'

Melville looked worried for her. It came out as a

villainous grimace, but Carol understood perfectly. Melville was sweet. Chrestomanci just looked surprised and a little bored. 'You mean you *want* all these people back?' he said.

Carol opened her mouth to say yes, of course she did! But she did not say it. They were having such fun. Bimbo was having the time of his life galloping through the streets throwing jewels. The people in the sea were a happy splashing mass, and waiters were hurrying about down in the square, taking orders and slapping down plates and glasses in front of the cast of thousands in the cafés. Carol just hoped they were using real money. If she turned her head, she could see that some of the cast of thousands had now got as far as the golf course, where most of them seemed to be under the impression that golf was a team game that you played rather like hockey.

'While Carol makes up her mind,' said Chrestomanci, 'what, Melville, is your personal opinion of her dreams? As one who has an inside view?'

Melville pulled his moustache unhappily. 'I was afraid you were going to ask me that,' he said. 'She has tremendous talent, of course, or she couldn't do it at all, but I do sometimes feel that she—well—she repeats herself. Put it like this: I think maybe Carol doesn't give herself a chance to be herself any more than she gives us.'

Melville, Carol realised, was the only one other people she really liked. She was heartily sick of all the others. Though she had not admitted it, they had bored her for years, but she had never had time to think of anyone more interesting, because she had always been so busy getting on with the next dream. Suppose she gave them all the sack? But wouldn't that hurt Melville's feelings?

'Melville,' she said anxiously, 'do you enjoy being villains?'

'My dear,' said Melville, 'it's up to you entirely, but I confess that sometimes I would like to try being someone . . . well . . . not black-hearted. Say, *grey*-hearted, and a little more complicated.'

This was difficult. 'If I did that,' Carol said, thinking about it, 'I'd have to stop dreaming for a while and spend a time—maybe a long time—sort of getting a new outlook on people. Would you mind waiting? It might take over a year.'

'Not at all,' said Melville. 'Just call me when you need me.' And he bent over and kissed Carol's hand, in his best and most villainous manner . . .

. . . And Carol was once again sitting up in her deck chair. This time, however, she was rubbing her eyes, and the terrace was empty except for Chrestomanci, holding a broken deck chair, and talking in what seemed to be Italian to a skinny little boy. The boy seemed to have come up from the bathing pool. He was wearing bathing trunks and dripping water all over the paving.

'Oh!' said Carol. 'So it was only a dream really!' She noticed she must have dropped her parasol while she was asleep and reached to pick it up. Someone seemed to have trodden on it. And there was a long trickle of fudge on her dress. Then of course she looked for her brooch, her pendant, and her bangles. They were gone. Someone had torn her dress pulling the brooch off. Her eyes leaped to the balustrade and found a small burnt saucepan standing on it.

At that, Carol jumped and ran to the balustrade, hoping to see Melville on his way down the stairs from the terrace. The stairs were empty. But she was in time to see Bimbo's cab, surrounded by gendarmes and stopped at the end of the parade. Bimbo did not seem to be in it. It looked as if he had worked the disappearing act she had invented for him in *The Cripple of Monte Christo.*

Down on the beach, crowds of the cast of thousands were coming out of the sea and lying down to sunbathe, or politely borrowing beach-balls from the other holidaymakers. She could hardly tell them from the regular tourists, in fact. Out on the golf links, the cast of thousands there was being sorted out by a man in a red blazer, and lined up to practise tee shots. Carol looked at the casino then, but there was no sign of Paul or Martha or Francis. Around the square, however, there was singing coming from the crowded cafés—steady, swelling singing, for, of course, there were several massed choirs among the cast of thousands. Carol turned and looked accusingly at Chrestomanci.

Chrestomanci broke off his Italian conversation in order to bring the small boy over by one wet, skinny shoulder. 'Tonino here,' he said, 'is a rather unusual magician. He reinforces other people's magic. When I saw the way your thoughts were going, I thought we'd better have him up to back up your decision. I suspected you might do something like this. That's why I didn't want any reporters. Wouldn't you like to come down to the pool now? I'm sure Janet can lend you a swimsuit and probably a clean dress as well.'

'Well . . . thank you . . . yes, please . . . but . . .' Carol began, when the small boy pointed to something behind her.

'I speaka Eengleesh,' he said. 'You droppa youra paper.'

Carol dived around and picked it up. In beautiful sloping writing, it said:

Carol Oneir hereby releases Francis, Lucy, Martha, Paul, and Bimbo from all further professional duties and gives the cast of thousands leave of indefinite absence. I am taking a holiday with your kind permission, and I remain
    Your servant,
      Melville.

'Oh good!' said Carol. 'Oh dear! What shall I do about Mr Ploys? And how shall I break it to Mama?'

'I can speak to Ploys,' said Chrestomanci, 'but your mama is strictly your problem, though your father, when he gets back from the casin—er, fishing—will certainly back you up.'

Dad did back Carol up some hours later, and Mama was slightly easier to deal with than usual anyway, because she was so confused at the way she had mistaken Chrestomanci's wife for a servant. By that time, however, the main thing Carol wanted to tell Dad was that she had been pushed off the diving board

sixteen times and had learned to swim two strokes—
well, almost.

*   *   *

DIANA WYNNE JONES has been described as 'a
modern mistress of magic' as the popularity of her
books in which magic and the mundane mingle have
skyrocketed on both sides of the Atlantic. Her series
of novels featuring Chrestomanci, 'The Most Powerful Magician in the World', have especially grown in
popularity ever since the first one, *Charmed Life*, was
published in 1977. In fact, there are lots of readers
who believe that the stories about the tall, handsome
and brilliant magician deserve the same cult status
as the Harry Potter novels. Diana Wynne Jones began
writing fantasy stories in 1970 and the titles of her
books soon revealed her fascination with wizards, and
witchcraft: *Witch's Business* (1974), *Howl's Moving
Castle* (1986) about the accursed Wizard Howl, and
A Sudden Wild Magic (1992) in which the secret
masters of the Earth are revealed to be a council of
male and female witches. Recently the *US News and
World Report* said, 'Mad about Harry? Try Diana', and
I would strongly recommend the other Chrestomanci
novels to new readers: *The Magicians of Caprona*
(1980), *Witch Week* (1982) and *The Lives of Christopher
Chant* (1988).

ACKNOWLEDGEMENTS

The editor and publishers are grateful to the following authors, their publishers and agents for permission to include copyright stories in this collection: 'School for the Unspeakable' by Manly Wade Wellman. Copyright © 1937 by Popular Fiction Publishing Company. Reprinted by permission of David Drake, successor to the Estate of Manly Wade Wellman.

'The Demon Headmaster' by Gillian Cross. Reprinted by permission of Oxford University Press.

'Ghostclusters' by Humphrey Carpenter. Copyright © 1989. Reprinted by permission of Puffin Books.

'Grimnir and the Shape-Shifter' by Alan Garner. Reprinted by permission of HarperCollins Publishers.

'Dark Oliver' by Russell Hoban. Reprinted by permission of David Higham Associates.

'Finders Keepers' by Joan Aiken. Copyright © Joan Aiken Enterprises Ltd and reprinted by permission of A. M. Heath & Co Ltd.

'The Magic of Flying' by Jacqueline Wilson. Reprinted by permission of Oxford University Press.

'Chinese Puzzle' by John Wyndham. Reprinted by permission of David Higham Associates.

'The Wish' by Roald Dahl. Reprinted by permission of David Higham Associates.

Invisible Boy' by Ray Bradbury. Reprinted by per-

mission of Abner Stein and Don Congdon Associates.
'My Name Is Dolly' by William F. Nolan. Copyright
© 1987 and reprinted by permission of the author.
'Something to Read' by Philip Pullman. Reprinted
by permission of A. P. Watt Ltd.
'Carol Oneir's Hundredth Dream' by Diana Wynne
Jones. Reprinted by permission of HarperCollins
Publishers.
With special thanks to Mike Ashley, David Drake,
William Nolan and Philip Pullman for their help in
assembling this collection.